A Song for Sarah

Lynette Sowell

Annie's®

AnniesFiction.com

Library of Congress-in-Publication Data
A Song for Sarah / by Lynette Sowell
p. cm.
I. Title
                          2018944143

AnniesFiction.com
(800) 282-6643
Hearts of Amish Country™
Series Creator: Shari Lohner
Series Editor: Jane Haertel

10 11 12 13 14 | Printed in China | 9 8 7 6 5 4 3

1

A red pickup truck left the two-lane back road and entered the driveway in front of the farm stand. Seated behind the truck's steering wheel was Katelynn Donnelly. Even from here, Sarah Stoltzfus could see her friend's wide smile.

The roar of the truck's engine ceased and a peaceful silence filled the late-August Tennessee air. Sarah much preferred the sound of the rhythm of horses' hooves and the jingle of the bit and harness to the sounds of the *Englisch* vehicles.

Katelynn sprang from the truck and shut the door with a *clunk*. Sarah couldn't help but smile at her friend's joy. Their lives couldn't be more different, but they had found a common love in gardening and now combined their efforts to run a roadside stand three days a week.

"You look very happy this morning," Sarah called out as Katelynn headed toward the stand.

"I am." Katelynn brushed her golden hair over her shoulder with her left hand, and a sparkle caught the morning light as she approached Sarah. For an English woman, Katelynn wasn't given to wearing much makeup or jewelry, something Sarah's parents approved of where the two young women's friendship was concerned. But Sarah knew what a ring on the third finger of a woman's left hand meant outside the Amish world.

"Oh, Katelynn—you're—?"

"Engaged!" Katelynn squealed, then clamped her hand over her mouth. "Steven proposed to me last night. I should have known something was up when I found out he was taking me to Riverbend for dinner. We had a table with a water view . . ." Her voice trailed off and a dreamy look crossed her face. "It was perfect."

"I'm so happy for you!" Sarah hugged her friend, then glanced at the glittering diamond. "It is a beautiful ring. If I owned such a ring, I'd be afraid of something happening to it." That, and it was very fancy and showy. She'd feel self-conscious with people staring at a bauble on her finger. Not that she'd never imagined herself wearing a bit of sparkle, more than the glint of a pin holding her plain, black apron in place.

"I'm a little nervous wearing it too. But only just a little." Katelynn pushed a few more strands of hair behind her ear, revealing simple golden hoop earrings.

There had been a few times Sarah had longed to wear earrings like that, but she questioned the idea of inflicting the pain of ear piercing on herself for vanity's sake, not to mention the attention she would draw, even if such adornments had been allowed. Still, *Gött* had created such beautiful things as diamonds and gold, and she could enjoy them from a distance.

"Have you chosen a wedding date? How long will it take you to plan everything?" English or Amish, Sarah knew from experience with other family members that weddings had a lot of details to plan.

"The weekend after Valentine's Day." Katelynn went back to the bed of her truck and pulled out a basket of green beans. "A little more than six months should be plenty of time. We're not planning anything too big or complicated. Or expensive."

"What about your schooling?" Sarah knew Katelynn was going to college to become a teacher, an admirable vocation. Marriage might put a crimp in those plans—at least it would for an Amish woman.

"I'll still finish on time. We can get married in February, take our honeymoon during spring break, and I can still keep up with my student teaching. It'll be busy, but I can handle it." Katelynn chuckled. "You sound like my mother, worrying about me. But I've got that much planned out, at least."

Sarah nodded and the two young women emptied the basket of green beans into one of the empty bins from which they sold the produce. Sarah's *Daed* had built the farm stand for them, with wood supplied by Katelynn's family. Together, they had painted the small building a bright white, inside and out, which showcased their produce beautifully.

She and Katelynn had decided to open the stand together after a chance meeting at the local general store in the tiny town of Apple Creek led to the discovery of their mutual love of gardening. Had it been only two years ago, when they were both purchasing seeds and gardening supplies on a rainy, late-winter morning? So much had happened since then.

Despite their different worlds, the two young women worked well together and spent time at the stand during the daylight hours of the late spring, all summer long, right through the final harvest in the fall.

Now it looked as though Katelynn's world would be diverging from Sarah's even more. Marriage changed people—Sarah had seen it happen when her sister married and moved to Wolfesboro, almost two hours away. The two sisters wrote letters to each other, which Sarah looked forward to despite the fact that the details of Emma's life with Jacob caused her some pain. Emma's correspondence had decreased as of late, but Sarah knew her sister was busy creating a new life in a new community.

Six months wasn't too short a time to plan a wedding, Sarah reflected as she checked the supply of paper bags for customers. Her family had made quick work of planning Emma's wedding to Jacob.

Those had been the longest four months of Sarah's life, from the time of the announcement of her sister's engagement to the ceremony.

Sarah didn't think anyone suspected her own feelings—that Jacob had passed Sarah by and that it had broken her heart. He'd married Emma instead.

Many times before the wedding, Sarah had wanted to ask Jacob for an explanation, but the time never seemed right. And by then, what difference would it have made? So the question was left unasked and would remain so. Only Gött knew the answer, and if she was meant to know, she supposed she'd find out someday. But in the meantime, well, her heart still hurt.

Sarah shoved the old thoughts aside and instead focused on Katelynn's present joy. During the space of time since Emma and Jacob's wedding, Sarah had been very busy, too busy to wallow in the past like a sad barnyard pig.

"Are you all right this morning, Sarah? You seem a bit more quiet than usual." Katelynn's face was etched with concern.

Sarah nodded. "Yes, I'm all right. I was just thinking about my sister, who lives in Wolfesboro. We were very close until she married almost two years ago. Even though it's not so very far away, I don't see her much, and I miss her."

I miss how things used to be . . . before Jacob.

"Change happens with friends and sisters. And anyway, you never know when big changes will come your way too." Katelynn touched Sarah's shoulder. "I promise you, we will still be friends after the wedding. I will still put in my garden next spring."

Sarah opened her mouth to say she didn't expect much to change for her anytime soon, but the *clip-clop* of hooves on the driveway made them both look up.

An Amish man, driving a two-seater buggy pulled by a dark-brown mare, slowed beside Katelynn's truck and continued to a nearby hitching post. Sarah couldn't recall having seen him before.

If she had, she knew she would have remembered him. A straw hat, slightly askew, sat atop hair the color of dark honey. He gave them a smile that she definitely would have remembered. He mopped his brow with the back of his hand and grinned at them as he hopped from the buggy.

"*Gut* morning," he said to them.

Katelynn nudged Sarah's elbow and whispered, "Here comes some change. Isn't he new?"

This had to be the nephew who'd recently moved to their community from Wolfesboro to help Abraham Miller with his farm. Or so she'd heard in a conversation her father was having with Bishop Hilty after the last Sunday worship gathering.

Abraham, a widower with no children, had been ill for a good part of the spring and this summer and needed help with chores and planting.

Sarah hadn't paid much attention to the information at the time, figuring she'd see the newcomer soon enough. He would be hard to miss. Their district was so small, only twenty-five families in all, not counting the two couples who were set to wed in the fall.

Sarah stood there, staring mutely at the new man, until she received another subtle jab in the arm from Katelynn's elbow.

Sarah ignored her. "*Gut* morning."

"*Gut* morning," the man replied, an amused expression on his face as he repeated himself. He surveyed the arrangement of vegetables, the jars of preserves lined up neatly on the front counter. Silence hung in the air, almost as thick as the humidity.

"I don't believe I've seen you here before," said Katelynn.

"No. Although, I have driven by several times. Decided to stop today." He wore no beard, which meant he wasn't married. And he was new here in Apple Creek. Sarah tamped down the interest that bloomed inside her, like a golden-yellow squash blossom. She knew nothing about this man.

"Well, we're certainly glad you did, Mister . . . ?" Katelynn's voice held a happy lilt.

Sarah felt her face flame, not from the humidity, but at her friend's boldness.

"I am Matthew Miller." He nodded to them. "I would like two jars of the blackberry preserves and one jar of apple butter. Do you have any bread?" He scanned the shelves.

"I'm afraid we don't, not this morning." Sarah's voice came out with a squeak, not unlike a mouse in the barn made after a cat cornered it. She cleared her throat. "But I can have some ready tomorrow, if you'd like."

"I would like, very much, please. I can come tomorrow to pick it up." He motioned to the bins containing produce that Sarah had picked less than an hour ago. "I will take some yellow squash and zucchini. And the smallest watermelon."

"When will you come by for the bread?"

"I can come after supper, before sundown. I will be in the fields tomorrow and may not get a break," said Matthew. "But fresh bread will be much better than my biscuits."

"Her bread is the best!" Katelynn nodded.

Sarah closed her eyes as she picked up the nearest basket of yellow squash and tucked four into a bag, after which she added the zucchini. She made passable bread and had been trying very hard to mimic her *Mamm*'s perfect loaves. She wouldn't say it was the best.

"Here you are." She held up the bag. "Eight dollars, please."

Matthew pulled a wallet from his pocket and fished out some bills, then handed them to Sarah. "*Danke*. I look forward to these vegetables for tonight's supper. Tomorrow I will be back for the bread. I'm sorry. I don't know your name."

"Sarah Stoltzfus," she managed.

"Tomorrow, Sarah Stoltzfus." Matthew gave both women a nod before striding away with a watermelon under one arm and the other clutching the bag of vegetables and preserves.

Katelynn smirked. "It's a good thing you don't have bread here today, because now he'll have to come back tomorrow. He's not married, is he? No beard?"

"No, I don't believe he is." A tiny weight seemed to lift from her troubled heart, then she mentally scolded herself. She needed to concentrate on her work and not on a pair of eyes the color of the bachelor's button flowers in the bouquets lining the front table.

Matthew let the horse set her own pace back to the farm after leaving the farm stand. The morning sun already beat down on them, promising as hot a day as yesterday. He almost longed for air-conditioning. Almost. Longing for something he could no longer have was pointless.

And proving himself to this new Amish district in which he lived meant he had to leave those conveniences behind him forever.

Now that he'd made the decision to return to the Amish life, part of him longed to be near the rest of his family in Wolfesboro. But for now, working his uncle Abraham's fields in the much smaller Amish community of Apple Creek—where there were fewer people who knew or cared about his history—would limit worldly distractions and help make his transition back into the Amish lifestyle easier. But at the moment, he didn't consider wanting a house with an interior temperature of seventy-five degrees to be a very worldly desire.

Abraham Miller was his father's brother and was nearing seventy years old. Widowed young, Abraham had never remarried, choosing obstinately instead to farm his land on his own. When the letter had arrived informing the family that Abraham had fallen ill and would need help, Matthew volunteered to be the one to head for Apple Creek and live with him.

Perhaps, in addition to proving he could be part of the community in Apple Creek, he would also be able to keep Abraham's farm in the family.

There was no way he could purchase the acreage on his own, unless Abraham would take payments for the land. Matthew had saved some money from his time living and working among the English, but it would only be enough for a good down payment on the property.

His *Rumspringa* had been a time of learning for him. It had had benefits, he couldn't deny, such as the freedom to do, say, and dress exactly as he pleased, to go wherever he wanted. And he'd stayed away much longer than most Amish young people—nearly ten years. But he had finally realized he was not meant to stay in the English world forever.

As the horse plodded along, Matthew recalled the wariness in the eyes of his family members upon his return a few months ago. He knew they all wondered if one day he might leave them again, and this time never come back.

He couldn't blame them. If he were in their shoes, he would wonder too. But they were wrong. He would not leave again unless he was forced out. He would do everything in his power to make everyone see that he was sincere in his desire—no, his *need*—to return to his roots.

Today Abraham was in Jackson, more than an hour away at a larger hospital than the local medical facility in Hardin County.

Abraham had collapsed the day before Matthew arrived in Apple Creek and had been seen by an English doctor—an extreme action on the family's part. The family agreed that Abraham could have the tests at the hospital, although like most Amish the Millers didn't normally seek medical opinions from the English. Surprisingly, the stubborn older man had agreed too.

"I will go for the tests, if you will leave me alone about them afterward," he'd said.

The family had hired an English driver to take him to his appointment. Abraham's eccentric Mamm, Matthew's grandmother who lived in Florida, insisted on the tests as well when someone had called her from an English phone and informed her of the news. Matthew was glad he was not the one who had had to relay that particular news to Abraham.

If Abraham could regain his good health, perhaps he would work his fields of soybeans once again. If not, well, Abraham had hesitantly agreed that he would *consider* going to the nearest *Daedi Haus* in Wolfesboro, where there was family and he could at least entertain himself by watching the tourists pass by the nearby farms. Somehow, Matthew couldn't see his uncle living that way. He wasn't *that* old.

Abraham had said as much over dinner the other evening. Matthew's Daed had made the trip from Wolfesboro, bringing a cooler of food to last several days. Matthew did love his Mamm's cooking.

But Matthew hadn't appreciated that his father had traveled to Apple Creek to meet with Abraham. Did he not trust him to make a good decision where Abraham was concerned?

After all, Matthew wasn't a child who needed minding, but a grown man of twenty-six. He suspected that his father's gruffness, though, was a cover for the fear that Matthew would leave again. His absence had left a large hole in the fabric of his father's trust. And of course Daed was worried about his brother.

"No, Daed, I won't disappoint you," he said aloud as he drove the buggy along the road flanked by fields that led to the two-story farmhouse. He surveyed the rows and rows of soybeans, their leaves bouncing with the slight breeze rippling over them.

Matthew wouldn't disappoint Abraham either. Right now he needed to check the fields and care for the animals. Then there was the fencing to repair at the rear of the property not far from the Tennessee River. He would have to see about hiring some help, likely one of the young local men not old enough to work their own land, but needing the money for their families.

His Daed had warned him that Abraham had a hard time keeping help, that the last workers on the farm had quit when better opportunities came that took them away from Apple Creek and off to Wolfesboro. Matthew couldn't help but wonder if Abraham's prickly demeanor had something to do with the workers' eagerness to find other employment.

Perhaps Levi Stoltzfus, who owned the neighboring farm, might know of someone. Or if not, Matthew could ask at the next Sunday meeting—at Bishop Hilty's house, in a few days.

The buggy hit a rock, causing two of the glass jars beside him on the seat to clink together. Matthew glanced down at his side and pulled open the top of the bag. The jars hadn't broken. Good. That would have been a waste of good jam made by a pretty young Amish woman. She must be Levi Stoltzfus's daughter.

His mouth watered at the thought of fresh bread topped with a pat of butter and a spoonful or two of the blackberry preserves. Well, the fresh bread would come tomorrow. Today he would make do with what Abraham had on hand.

Matthew didn't need to tell the horse, who bore the rather obvious name of Brown, to slow down as they approached the driveway to the

Miller farm. He had gotten an early start this morning on his errand to buy supplies to repair the fence. It had been his first solo trip driving to Apple Creek and back, not quite five miles round trip. Driving a buggy had come back to him quickly in the few weeks he'd been back among his people.

The horse turned into the driveway, barely flicking her tail when a car shot past them, its driver blaring the horn.

Now *that* was what he couldn't abide from the English and had never gotten used to in the outside world. Rudeness. Matthew halted the buggy in front of the barn door and hopped from the seat.

"Here we go, Brown." He began the process of unhitching the horse. Unhitching and harnessing a horse again had taken a few tries, but he now had it down pat. Brown gave a flick of her ear in approval of Matthew's technique.

Matthew's thoughts drifted back to the farm stand. And to that pretty young Amish woman, Sarah. She intrigued him. The top of her head came just to the level of his shoulder. Her hair, dark as chocolate, was pulled back neatly and covered by her simple *Kapp*. She wore a white head covering for summer, as most of the ladies did, while he and the rest of the men wore straw hats. For winter, both the white and straw would be replaced by the black, as soon as the first frost appeared on the fields. It was their community's tradition.

Yet her eyes were what intrigued him the most. Almond-shaped and deep brown, topped by expressive brows, they lit up when she smiled, but he thought he'd detected a sadness. A buried, old pain? Maybe he saw it in her only because he carried his own.

At any rate, he looked forward to seeing her again and to getting some fresh bread. If it was one thing his people could make well, it was bread. When he was out in the world, just walking by an English bakery and inhaling the aroma would bring him back to the taste of what he remembered. But it had never tasted the same. Nothing ever had.

Matthew reminded himself, however, that his season here in Apple Creek might be only just that—a season. He'd found his way back to the plain people, to the hats and suspenders, to the slower pace. But what was his true place here? Helping his family might help him figure that out.

2

"A new man stopped at the farm stand today," Sarah announced as soon as she and Mamm had cleared away the supper dishes. "I think he's the nephew of Abraham Miller that's come from Wolfesboro to help on the farm. His name is Matthew Miller."

Daed nodded from his spot at the head of the table. He took a sip of coffee, something he drank morning, noon, and night, no matter the weather.

"*Jah*, he and his father met with the bishop, and with Abraham." Her father set his cup down with a firm clunk. "It's *gut* that Abraham will have help. Although he is stubborn and does not want to hire someone, he might otherwise lose his crop without it."

Mamm took her seat across from Sarah. "Do you think this is his last season to farm?"

"It is hard to say. He told me once he might sell. I have my eye to buy the property, unless some other Miller steps up. Abraham seems wary of them, though. But he's always been a bit different."

"*Ach*, more property, Levi? You are not so young as you once were." Mamm's words were warm, yet truthful.

"Well, this is what has today made me think more seriously of buying that farm." Daed pulled an envelope from his shirt pocket. "A letter from Emma and Jacob."

A letter! Sarah almost wanted to reach across the table and snatch up the envelope, to see what news her sister had to share. She felt the ripple of an old ache in her heart and ignored it. Instead, her curiosity was piqued. It had been at least four weeks since hearing from her sister, when it used to be they would share secrets morning, noon, and night.

"What does a letter have to do with Abraham Miller's property?" Sarah spoke first.

"Your sister and her husband are talking about moving back here, to Apple Creek. If they—we—bought Abraham's property, it would be extremely beneficial for all of us. We could work the land, side by side, as a family."

A lump formed in Sarah's throat. Emma and Jacob, coming back *here*? For good?

"But—but they are happy in Wolfesboro," Sarah observed. "Emma with her quilt sales, and Jacob making cabinets."

Part of Sarah rejoiced at the idea of her sister returning. But she couldn't deny it had been something of a relief having her and Jacob living away from Apple Creek, where she wouldn't have to see them every day and be reminded every day of her disappointment at not being Jacob's choice. Yet she had to admit that in that time some of that disappointment had softened, though she couldn't have said why. Perhaps it was Gött working on her heart.

"I can think of a few reasons why a woman might want to live closer to her Mamm," Sarah's mother said softly.

A realization dawned on Sarah. Her sister must be having a child. Of course a married woman would want and need to be near her mother, especially the first time.

"Yes, I believe I can think of at least one reason." Sarah stood, reaching for her empty plate and collecting her parents' plates, then heading for the sink. Scrubbing the supper dishes would give her hands something to do while she processed her Daed's announcement.

So, it looked as though she would be an *Aenti* again. At twenty-two, Sarah was the only one left in the family home with their parents.

Her brother and three sisters were married with homes of their own, all in Wolfesboro, all except Emma busy raising their own growing broods of children. More than once she'd felt the gentle glances from her mother, seen the questioning looks from the other women. There were so few eligible young men in Apple Creek. Would Sarah be an old maid, destined to care for other peoples' children, or her parents in their old age?

Sarah turned on the faucet to prepare the water for dishes. Thankfully, her father had installed a propane heater that warmed the water. Gone were the days of her childhood when they would have to heat water on the stove. Her father had conceded to her mother's requests and the kitchen had run much more smoothly with the convenience.

A faint breeze ruffled the curtains framing open windows where a battery-operated fan sat, its blades whirling. The device came out only on the warmest days. Today, Sarah basked in the slight breeze it offered.

She heard her father say something about going out to check the animals, and he left the table and then the house. Looking through the window, she saw him crossing the yard in the direction of the barn. Mamm joined her at the sink.

"Yes, your sister will be having a child. December, right before Christmas." Her Mamm wrapped the leftovers from the meal, which would serve as lunch for them the following day. "If Abraham Miller sells the property this autumn and all goes well with that, Emma and Jacob could be moved in before the baby is born."

Sarah nodded. She felt out of place in her own home. She should have a home of her own, be standing at her own sink, watching her own husband walk across her own yard. The sink filled with water, the soap foaming up around the plates.

Her mother's voice pulled her from her thoughts.

"I know it was hard for you, after Emma was betrothed to Jacob." Mamm's words were gentle, her tone low. "Do you think you will have difficulty, knowing they might be living next door, being our neighbors?"

"I admit it was hard for me at first, especially when Emma and Jacob began courting. But that was quite a long time ago." Sarah rinsed the supper plates and set them on the rack to dry. "With the two of them being gone as long as they have, it's become easier. If they live next door to us, I'll be fine. I'd love to have Emma close by again. But it's possible Abraham will not sell."

"Maybe." Mamm gave her a sideways glance. "How did the produce stand fare today?"

"Very good. I'll have enough money to buy more quilt fabric, and then maybe we can start piecing another quilt soon, depending on when we finish the one we're working now." A thought struck her. "I do need to bake some sourdough bread tonight, for tomorrow. Matthew Miller came by the stand, looking for some bread and I had none."

"Well, we can take him a loaf of ours tonight rather than wait for tomorrow. I'll go with you." Mamm nodded. "We should welcome him to Apple Creek, and we can check on Abraham at the same time."

"Yes, a welcome would be a neighborly thing to do." Sarah's heart fluttered before she willed it down. They were only talking about a loaf of bread, for heaven's sake.

The two made quick work of the remainder of the dishes, then Mamm handed her a basket and a small towel. "Tuck the bread into this towel. I'll get some butter too, in case they have not made time to churn. I am not sure that Abraham has much set up in his house, not like a woman would, anyway."

They strode off together, down the dirt lane to the end of the driveway, then onto the narrow asphalt road. Sarah longed for autumn as the heat shimmered from the pavement. Dirt roads didn't shed heat like this. If a rainstorm were to come up, no doubt the road would steam.

Her mother fanned herself with her hand. "Perhaps we should have taken the buggy, even if it is only the next farm over. I didn't think about how warm it is, with the sun not set."

"That would have been a good idea." Sarah had been going to suggest taking the buggy to the Millers, but she assumed that her father would think it frivolous and a waste of time, when they both had perfectly strong enough legs to carry them the short distance.

Mamm spoke excitedly, all along the way, of the addition of another grandchild to the family. Presently there were nine, but ten would be even better, she said.

Sarah agreed. "Babies are a blessing."

Someday, she'd get her turn. But she didn't want to marry only for the sake of marriage and a baby. Marriage was for life, and even among the plain people, not all marriages were happy ones.

"I know we haven't talked about it in a while," her mother said as they rounded the corner of Abraham Miller's driveway, "but trust Gött. He will make a way for His will."

"I suppose you're right. But I have not been looking. There really isn't anyone here in our district that I am interested in."

No one had tried to match Sarah up with anyone, not lately. Truthfully, there were "slim pickings," as her best friend, Lydia Fry, also unmarried, was fond to say. Most Apple Creek young women knew they would likely end up marrying someone from Wolfesboro and moving there.

"Anyway," Mamm continued, "you are still very young. Marriage is nothing to rush. If there was, I would encourage you to go to Wolfesboro, to work in a store there. Or I imagine you could open your own quilt shop in Wolfesboro and live with your brother and his family. I'm sure they wouldn't mind the extra hands to help with the children in the meantime."

Sarah didn't want to help with anyone else's children. But the idea of having her own store, where she could sell quilts, sewing supplies, and the like . . . that was worth considering.

"I would like a shop. But I'd rather have it here in our community and not so far away. For now, the farm stand is good enough."

"I must say, I wasn't sure that working a farm stand with that young English woman would be a wise idea. I didn't see it lasting more than a season, at the most. But she seems to work very hard and you both get along well. So, I'm glad for you."

"Well, things may be changing, where the stand is concerned. Katelynn is now engaged to be married, she told me today. I wondered at first if she would continue the stand next year, after she marries in February. But she said she will."

"Ah, maybe her new husband will not care for the idea, after the wedding. Once a woman marries, her focus should be on her household and husband. More things than a garden and books. And isn't she going to college? After she is through with her education, it will take her away." Mamm shook her head.

"You're probably right about that. She is going to be a schoolteacher. I can't imagine her fiancé would object, though."

Sarah and her mother finally reached the Millers' farmhouse. A few more steps, and they headed up the front porch steps to the white farmhouse. The screen door allowed a glimpse into a dimly lit, sparsely furnished sitting room, with a kitchen beyond.

A figure, backlit from the open windows at the rear of the house, rose from a chair to approach the screen door. Matthew.

"Good afternoon, Sarah. This is a nice surprise." He nodded to her Mamm.

"I am Beatrice Stoltzfus, Sarah's Mamm."

"I am pleased to meet you." He opened the door and joined them on the porch.

When he'd said their arrival was a surprise, he'd meant it. In the time Matthew had been here, Abraham had had only a handful of visitors.

"We've brought you a little something to help welcome you to Apple Creek. We should have brought it sooner," Sarah's mother announced.

Sarah held up a basket she clutched in both hands.

"Thank you very much." Matthew took the basket from Sarah. A quick flicker of her eyes up at him was followed by a pretty flush to her cheeks. Mrs. Stoltzfus's cheeks had a rosy glow as well, probably from the exertion of the walk in this heat.

"I was going to start baking bread tonight, as promised, but my Mamm suggested we bring some over to you instead. We also brought some butter. What goes better with bread than butter?" Sarah smiled.

"I'd say some of that delicious jam I purchased from you today," Matthew said. At that, the flush in Sarah's cheeks deepened. "Thank you, both of you, very much."

"So how is Abraham doing?" Mamm asked.

"The hospital in Jackson decided to keep him overnight for one test tomorrow morning first thing, which I understand he is not happy about."

"If you need any help keeping house, Sarah and I will be happy to provide assistance. I'm sure you are quite busy with the farm." Mrs. Stoltzfus nodded firmly.

"Danke. It is good to have you as neighbors. I wasn't certain what

I had agreed to at first, but now that I have had a chance to see how Abraham is living, I'm not sure that continuing to live alone is the best idea for him."

He saw the unanswered questions in both of their eyes, why an unmarried man of Matthew's age wasn't set up yet at a farm or working a trade. He knew the questions would eventually come, and not just from his new neighbors, but from the rest of the Apple Creek community. He wondered when the stories or rumors might come about his years among the English, as well. So far, they had not. But he'd been there less than a week.

Sarah was the first to continue the conversation. "We'll be praying for him and for you, as you try to help him. I don't know whether you have a garden set up here for the summer, but I'm glad to share extra produce with you both."

"But your farm stand—"

"No. You and Abraham are our neighbors, and that's how we do things here in Apple Creek," Sarah insisted.

"Well, danke again." He couldn't help but grin at her earnest tones. "I'm not sure about Abraham's tastes, but I'm not particularly fond of beets. Although, I do appreciate whatever you have to give us."

"No beets. I'll be sure to remember that."

The sound of a buggy made him look past their shoulders. A plain man approached, driving a black buggy pulled by a dark-brown, almost black, horse.

Bishop Hilty.

"Ah, I see you have company," Sarah's mother said, glancing toward the driveway. "We shall leave now."

"Thank you for coming by, and for the offers of help and the food." As they left, Matthew realized, in spite of himself, that he wanted to know more about Sarah Stoltzfus.

She was curious, enterprising. Not nearly as forward as most of the women he'd encountered while among the English. Which was a good thing. Yet not so passive she wouldn't speak her mind. He liked that, and the fact that she clearly cared for people.

Matthew watched the two women exchange greetings with the bishop before continuing along the driveway. The bishop climbed down from the buggy and headed in his direction. The older man adjusted his suspenders as he ambled along, clad in his formal black coat despite the late summer heat. This was not purely a social call, Matthew suspected.

He met the bishop at the white picket fence that bordered the little yard. "Bishop. Hello." He inclined his head slightly as he spoke.

"Matthew. I've come to see how you and your uncle are."

"I am doing well. Abraham is having tests at the hospital in Jackson." Matthew motioned toward the house. "Would you like something to drink? Water, coffee? I know it is a warm evening, but I can heat the coffee."

"No, danke."

"I was preparing to feed the animals and bring the cow in for the evening."

"I will come with you."

The old sensation, one of the reasons he'd felt compelled to leave his people before, was the near constant scrutiny of actions, whether merely innocent or questionable. Maybe, though, the bishop was visiting purely out of kindness and concern.

On the other hand, he'd gauged the Stoltzfus women's visit. He didn't know about Sarah, but he was pretty sure her mother had been satisfying her own curiosity about the new unmarried neighbor.

But a matchmaking mother was the least of his worries at the moment. The person who could have him sent away from here—forever—was walking by his side.

They headed toward Abraham's barn. Matthew already knew the structure needed a new roof. He intended to see to the repairs before the autumn rains came—if he was here that long. With each day that passed, he more and more thought his place was to stay on this farm.

As if reading his thoughts, the bishop asked, "How long do you intend to live with Abraham?" The bishop gave him an unwavering look. Matthew didn't flinch. The man's expression wasn't challenging, but it was questioning. Bishop didn't beat around the bush, either. Matthew appreciated that.

"I'll stay here until the rest of the family decides that Abraham doesn't need help anymore, whether that is sooner or later. I know he doesn't want to leave the farm, but I also know the time is coming, and is likely here already, when he won't be able to handle the work. Not just until he 'feels better,' but permanently."

"He is an opinionated man." Bishop Hilty nodded, stroking his gray beard. The bishop was about the same age as Matthew's own father, who was in his early sixties.

"My Daed told me it is hard for a man to know when it is time to let another make decisions for himself. We have talked about plans for my own mother and father's future care as well, though they are both in excellent health." Matthew stopped at the gate which led to the cow pasture. The cow and a calf born in the spring waited patiently for him, but the cow let out a soft moo, probably needing to be milked. Matthew let the animals into the barn, where they ambled to the stall they shared.

"What are your intentions toward our fellowship? I am aware that you lived in the Wolfesboro district before you came here. But you have not been baptized."

Ah. There it was. Matthew had known the question would come. "No, Bishop Hilty. I was not a full member of that fellowship, and I had not been baptized. I had been—away—for some years before returning to Wolfesboro. Nine, to be exact. I came back in January and was proving myself to the community."

Matthew kept himself composed and took a deep breath as he headed for the outdoor water pump and filled a bucket.

The bishop trailed along with him as Matthew fed and watered the animals, then securely locked the gates. At last, the older man continued.

"I understand also that you are not married. And there are no prospects awaiting you, back in Wolfesboro?"

"No. Right now there is no one I intend to court. I have struggled with many things about myself. My faith. How I let my family and my community down."

Please, God, don't let him ask me anything about Rebecca. Because I'm not sure what I can explain that would make me feel less guilty.

Matthew and the bishop headed back toward the house. He let the bishop take the lead in the conversation.

"That is a *gut* thing, that you are thinking about such matters." Bishop Hilty nodded. "Because I was going to tell you, if you are not certain about how long you will be in our community, I suggest that you restrain any inclination you might have for finding a wife among our young women here in Apple Creek."

Bishop Hilty paused where they stood, halfway between the barn and the house. "We have but a few women of marrying age here. For our community's sake, I do not want them to marry and leave. Although, I have no real say in the matter. I'm thinking of our district and our fellowship. We are trying to build the district here in Apple Creek, not have members leave us, one by one. Even if they remain plain in another community."

Matthew had to nod at that. It made sense. "I understand, and I agree. That's why, for now, I've decided it would not be fair to pursue a woman in this community if I am not to be here permanently. I do want to find my place here."

He knew to tread carefully where bishops were concerned. Long ago, he had been responsible for one woman leaving the Wolfesboro community. And because of that, she'd never been back and probably never would be now.

Matthew didn't confess any of these things to the bishop, but he'd spoken to Rebecca Mast's family upon his return to Wolfesboro earlier this year. They'd wept and forgiven him. He'd struggled with forgiving himself. He still did.

The bishop nodded slowly. Perhaps Matthew had said the right thing, for once, though it was nothing but the truth.

"Very good." The bishop scanned the roofline of the barn and then the other outbuildings. "I can see that Abraham needs help. We will announce at the next Sunday gathering that we will plan a day to repair the roof, if you think Abraham will be agreeable to it."

"I know the repairs are definitely needed, and I would welcome the help, whether Abraham does or not. It's something I've planned to do, but hadn't gotten around to it just yet while I've attended to Abraham and some other items around the house that needed fixing."

"All right, then. We will organize something after you gather a list of the materials, and we will all set to work."

"Danke, Bishop." He watched as the man strode to his waiting buggy and horse.

The feeling of community comforted Matthew. It was one of the best things about the Amish, his people, the way they took care of each other.

But what had he gotten himself into, coming here? He'd thought

Apple Creek would be a better place to start over than in Wolfesboro. Fewer prying eyes and less speculation about his past.

But it looked like there was plenty of that going on here, too.

3

At least a dozen fresh cucumbers, nearly a bushel of tomatoes, a few pounds of potatoes, and the first good ears of corn bounced in the small handcart Sarah pulled to the farm stand at the edge of the driveway.

Before the sun had slipped over the treetops that Saturday morning, Sarah had walked through row after row of her garden to pick the freshest, ripest produce, which would be gone by early afternoon. Regular customers knew to come early, and the first of the vehicles would be stopping at the farm stand before long.

The remainders of yesterday's produce had vanished from the small outside shelf, upon which also rested a metal cashbox with a slit cut in the top, bolted to the stand. At the end of business each day, Sarah would leave the rest of the produce on the shelf and customers would follow the directions on a small hand-printed price list. Using the honor system had worked well.

Sarah paused long enough to glance at the empty shelf and the cashbox before she opened the wooden shutters that closed to cover the stand's windows after produce sales were done.

Something, though, caught her attention and made her pause for a closer look. Was that a dent on the cashbox?

Sarah released her hold on the cart's handle and stepped toward the box, which was outfitted with a padlock.

She fished the key from her apron pocket and opened the box. Inside was about ten dollars in bills and change, she estimated. Tucking the cash into her apron pocket, she relocked the cashbox.

She closed the box's lid and studied the lock. The padlock fitted through metal loops, one on the box's lid and one attached to the base, with the lock keeping the contents of the box secure.

But fresh, bright marks on the metal told her someone had struck the box with something hard, leaving scrapes behind.

Someone had tried to open the box without the key. A thief?

Sarah ran her fingers over the marks. The thought troubled her.

The honor-system box brought in at least seventy-five dollars per week on top of the other produce sales, which were split between her and Katelynn. Sarah didn't want to suspect anyone of trying to open the box, but the shiny marks on the dull metal told her it had to be true.

Until now, there had never been a problem with leaving the cashbox on the stand overnight. Should she and Katelynn stop using it, even though it would cut into their profits? She would be glad to give any extra produce—except for beets—to the Millers next door, now that she was better aware of their situation. And if someone needed that money, truly needed it, she wouldn't mind helping them. But a thief?

A sudden flash of light on metal made her look toward the road, where a blue pickup truck approached the stand, then pulled into the parking area. Sarah fanned herself with one hand. Maybe she and Katelynn would close down early today. Or maybe Katelynn would bring a fan. She had a small one that she could plug into her truck.

An English man approached. Young, but not very many years older than herself, she guessed. He smiled at her like he knew her. It was a smile not too different from the one Jacob used to give her, when she thought she was special to him. On this stranger, the smile didn't make her feel special. It made her wrap her arms around her waist and take a step back from him.

"Mornin'." The man nodded at her, his grin widening. "You seen Katelynn yet?"

"No. But she should be here any moment." Sarah scanned the roadway. "Are you a friend of hers?"

"Naw, I'm just the royal pain in her backside."

The young man stepped closer, extending his hand in her direction. Locks of his hair, long even for an English man, fell across one eye. "Keith Donnelly. I'm Katie-bug's big brother."

Sarah shook his hand. Keith Donnelly held her hand a bit longer than necessary, but she wrested it away gently. "Nice to meet you."

She wished she could say the same, but kept her uncharitable thoughts to herself.

"Well, like I said, Katelynn should be here soon." She motioned to the farm stand. "I'm not sure where she is, but you're welcome to wait until she arrives."

Keith glanced at the produce brimming at the top of Sarah's cart. "Need a hand unloading this? I can help."

Sarah paused for a second. She didn't really need any help, but if it would keep this man from staring at her, well, he could unload produce all he wanted. Keeping him occupied would make her a lot more comfortable.

"All right. Though there's not much to unload just yet. This is my first trip from the garden this morning. I'll get more after your sister arrives with her produce and can take over the stand." She opened the nearest set of shutters, revealing the interior, which was set up like a miniature market.

She'd thought the design quite clever, and her father had used her own drawing as a guide when he built it. She felt rather proud too, that both she and Katelynn had pooled their funds to purchase the wood. It was a shed with a door and large open windows on each side that let in light and air in the daytime, with shutters that closed and latched at night. It was wrong to think herself clever, or to be proud, she reminded herself. But surely it wasn't wrong that having her own little business pleased her?

Sarah then opened the farm stand's door and sunlight poured into the building. She entered the space and checked the tags on the empty baskets. The potatoes she'd brought wouldn't fill the basket, but maybe Katelynn would bring more from her garden. She felt Keith's eyes on her as he approached.

"Katie's told me about the setup you two have here." Keith paused in the doorway. He held a box of tomatoes and looked at the interior of the stand. "I'm really impressed. She told me y'all really make bank here in the summers. But then, she's always been the one with all the ambition and git-go."

Sarah nodded. "We do very well here. You're right, your sister is a hard worker."

"That she is." He chuckled before continuing. "I like to say, I'm either workin' hard or hardly workin'."

Keith Donnelly wasn't a very tall man, but he definitely seemed larger—and too close—within the confines of the stand.

Sarah cleared her throat and rubbed her neck as she did so. "Just set the box down here." She indicated a spot on a table. "I'll put them in the bins." The last thing she needed was this man bruising the delicate, ripe tomatoes. Where was Katelynn?

The familiar *clip-clop* of hooves on pavement filled her with relief. Not Katelynn, then, but she didn't care who it was at the moment. She just hoped whoever it was would stop at the stand to buy potatoes. Or jam. Or to buy anything at all. It didn't matter. She stepped past Keith and out into the sunshine.

A wave of relief washed over her when she saw Matthew Miller holding the reins from where he sat in the buggy.

When he caught sight of her, his brow furrowed and he urged

the horse to trot a bit faster. He reined to a halt, stopping the buggy beside the gleaming blue truck.

"*Gut* morning, Sarah." Hopping from the buggy, Matthew tossed the reins on the seat as he did so. "I'm stopping for a moment on my way to town."

"Matthew, it is good to see you this morning. Very good to see you." She said his name loud enough that she was sure Keith would hear.

"Do you have any corn picked yet?" Matthew asked. He glanced at Keith, who stepped out of the shed and came to stand beside her.

"Jah, a few ears. There's not much to pick just yet. But you're welcome to what we have now." She gestured toward Keith. "This is Katelynn's brother." She didn't know if Matthew knew or cared who Katelynn's brother was, but she felt the urge to explain.

"Hello." Matthew nodded at Keith. The two appeared to assess each other, as if they were two roosters facing off in the farmyard.

Keith nodded in return. He looked at Sarah. "Katie said she was going to be here by eight, and it's almost eight thirty. I'm burnin' daylight and gotta get to a job. They won't pay me to stand around here talking to a pretty young lady."

"I'll tell her you stopped by." Sarah tried to ignore the "pretty young lady" remark and tried harder not to frown. Katelynn wasn't usually late on the days they worked the stand together.

Keith shrugged and strode over to his truck. "Have her call me, would you? I'm trying not to blow up her phone, but she didn't answer a few minutes ago. It's kinda important."

Once behind the wheel of the vehicle, he gunned the engine, causing Matthew's horse to rear up its head, its ears pinned back.

Matthew dashed for the horse's head, then grabbed the reins. The horse had taken a few backward steps, but Matthew held firm to the reins. He stroked the animal's nose and talked to it in low tones.

"Sorry, dude!" Keith called out as he backed the truck away from the stand. The truck sped off, engine roaring. The sound grew softer as the truck disappeared from view.

Sarah let out the breath she'd been holding. "I do not like that man," she heard herself saying aloud.

Matthew hurried back to her side. "He was bothering you, wasn't he?"

"Not really." She struggled to find the right words. "He just . . . he made me feel . . . I don't know. I can't explain. But I'm glad you're here. Thank you for stopping. Would you like the corn?"

He nodded. "Yes. I'll get it on the way back from town."

Sarah appreciated the fact that he didn't ask any more questions about Keith or how uncomfortable he'd made her feel. Jacob had been the first man she had felt an interest in, and she could no longer have feelings toward him. But now she let herself look at Matthew's expression. Kindness, concern, curiosity—and perhaps a hint of a little more? Yet guarded.

Sarah understood guarded very well.

She was a silly girl, she told herself as Matthew began unloading the rest of the produce into the stand. She'd only encountered this man three times and there was no indication, really, that he had any real interest in her. He hadn't even proven himself to the district and been officially accepted by the community. That could take six months, or longer, depending on how things went.

Just then, Katelynn's red pickup pulled up and came to a stop. She wore an apologetic expression as she hopped from the driver's side of her truck.

"I'm so sorry. I had a flat tire when I left the bank, and I needed some help getting it changed." She smiled at seeing Matthew there at the stand. "Well, good morning, Mr. Miller."

"Your brother, Keith, was just here to see you. He left a few minutes ago," Sarah blurted. "I'm surprised you didn't pass him on the road."

At Sarah's words, Katelynn sighed, shook her head, closing her eyes. "He didn't ask you for money, did he?"

"No. He said he was supposed to meet you here at eight. I told him you would be arriving soon. But then he left suddenly, saying he had to go to a job."

Katelynn opened her mouth as if she was about to say more, then appeared to change her mind. "I'll call him after I get the truck unloaded."

Katelynn had mentioned that her brother had moved back in with the family earlier that summer, but hadn't said much about it, and this was the first time Sarah had met him in person.

Sarah nodded. "I need to go back for my second cart of vegetables."

Matthew hesitated, as if he would move to join Katelynn at the rear of her truck. But Katelynn waved him off.

"I can get this myself, thanks. If you'd like to give Sarah a hand with the garden. I'm sure she'll be glad for the help." Her eyes sparkled.

Sarah stepped toward the handcart, but Matthew beat her to it and grabbed the handle. She tried not to give Katelynn a look. Her friend acted as if she were an old-woman matchmaker. It was a bit humorous, but Sarah hadn't shaken off Keith's "creep factor," a term she'd heard Katelynn use a time or two when referring to an unsavory customer.

"Come, I'll show you the garden." Sarah motioned for Matthew to follow her back up the driveway.

This morning, Matthew hadn't planned to be ambling along the Stoltzfus driveway toward the rows and rows of vegetables that made up Sarah's garden, but here he was, tugging a handcart as he did so.

Sarah glanced up at him as they walked side by side. "Thank you for your help. It'll go more quickly with an extra pair of hands." A bead of sweat crept along her brow and she swiped it away. She led him to the rows of tomato plants, their pungent scent tickling his nostrils.

"You are very welcome." Despite the bishop's warning about the unmarried women of Apple Creek, Matthew allowed himself to wonder about Sarah. "Your garden must be a profitable business."

"Yes. It's definitely been worth the effort. My Daed was skeptical when I asked him for help in building the stand, but I've shown him that both plain and English alike will pay for good products. Katelynn and I split the money. I use mine for quilting supplies. The ladies in the district gather here to make quilts. We send one to the Haiti Benefit Auction in Sarasota, Florida, every year." She stopped along the first row of tomato plants, studded with plump tomatoes in varying shades of red and green.

He smiled at the mention of Florida. Now, that place had some very good memories for him. "Sarasota is wonderful. Have you ever visited Pinecraft?" he asked, referring to the Amish and Mennonite community in the midst of a very English city. "My *Grossmammi* lives there part of the year, and I stayed with her for a time a couple of years ago."

"No, I haven't. For one thing, Bishop Hilty speaks against it and says that taking 'vacations' is a frivolous use of time." Sarah shrugged as she picked a fat green tomato from a nearby plant.

"I see." Matthew again reminded himself that he'd returned to this district willingly. But everyone, Amish and English alike, deserved a vacation once in a while.

Sarah glanced toward the field of lettuce where her father walked behind his team of horses as they plowed under a field of plants which had already lived out their purpose. Despite the distance between them and her father, she lowered her voice.

"But I have to say, I've always wanted to visit Pinecraft. I don't think visiting would be a bad thing. And to see the ocean! What it must be like, so beautiful and blue and wide." Her voice took on a longing tone. "I don't believe it is a bad thing to want to see and appreciate God's creation."

"The ocean, the Gulf of Mexico, is indeed very beautiful. The sand is white, white as flour against the blue of the water and the sky. The weather is always beautiful in Pinecraft too." They continued walking along the tomato plants. Matthew stopped and pointed at one plant, its branches drooping under the weight of the tomatoes. "Green ones only, right now?"

"Yes. I sell out of green tomatoes quickly, every morning. Fried green tomatoes are a local favorite." Sarah tapped one tomato, half green and half red. "I'll let this one ripen."

They continued to walk along, picking green tomatoes here and there.

"So, what is Pinecraft, the community itself, really like?" Sarah asked. "I have a hard time imagining being plain in a city, with so many noisy cars and trucks, and buildings. And no farms."

"In the winter, Pinecraft is very busy. There are singings and barbecues. Shuffleboard and boccie for the older people. The younger people go to the beach and play volleyball. It's also a honeymoon spot, for newlyweds." At that, Matthew cleared his throat. "There are quite a few plain churches there too, that stay very busy with services, Old and New Orders, and Mennonite."

"I have to say, it does sound like very good fun, like a Sunday afternoon every day. But how do people live there all the time? Surely they don't sit idle or just amuse themselves."

"No, they don't. Many are older and watch the homes for their families. The younger people clean houses, or build things and work construction. And there are also shops and restaurants catering to the tourists."

"It sounds like Wolfesboro in a way, but a lot bigger."

"Sort of," Matthew explained. "Not too many people live there year-round. Most people take buses from Indiana, Illinois, and Pennsylvania to get there. Even a few from here in Tennessee. My grandmother hires someone to drive her back and forth from Wolfesboro."

Sarah nodded slowly. "Maybe this winter, instead of shipping the quilt to Florida, I could find a way to bring it there myself and stay for the auction . . . but that would be silly and wasteful to spend the money, when shipping it is cheaper. I couldn't go there alone anyway. Bishop says vacations are idleness, a foolish frittering of time."

Sarah picked another tomato, adding it to the few she carried in her apron. She glanced toward the handcart behind them. Matthew moved to pull the cart closer to where they stood, taking care not to drop his armful of tomatoes as he did so.

Ah, the bishop again. The man's warning yesterday still didn't sit well with him. Was it because Matthew, in his heart, was already rebelling against authority—something that was clearly a sin?

"What do you think? Is this enough tomatoes?" Matthew glanced at the cart, then toward the next row of plants, zucchini and yellow squash peeking out at them from under leafy vines.

"For now." Sarah joined him. She moved the tomatoes from her apron, depositing them into the cart, then followed Matthew's gaze. "Next will be the squash. I sell more tomatoes and squash than anything else."

They moved on and Matthew continued their discussion. "So what would prevent you from going to Pinecraft to visit, besides the bishop's warnings? Why couldn't you go alone and hire a woman to drive you? Maybe you could ride with my grandmother and you could share the expenses." Matthew regretted asking the questions as soon as they'd come out of his mouth. Being among the English for the time he had, he'd grown accustomed to unmarried women coming and going as they pleased, even traveling great distances unaccompanied.

"Because my place is here and, like I said, it would take too much time and money, going to Florida even for a few days." She almost sounded wistful, as if she were trying to convince herself, despite her own objections. "Where did you live, before Wolfesboro, if you weren't in Pinecraft?"

"I met some people from Ohio while I was in Florida. They promised me a job at a Mennonite cabinet company. So I left Florida and went to Ohio to work for a few years, before I decided to come back to Tennessee." Matthew pushed the cart a few more steps down the row of low-lying squash plants.

"Moving here and there. I don't think I would like that." Sarah shook her head.

"I suppose I did," Matthew said. "For a while. The more I was with the people I met from Ohio, the more I realized I missed my family here. And I missed being Amish, though it took me a long time to realize that. So after Christmas this past year, I decided to come home to Tennessee once and for all."

"I am certain they're very happy you're here." Sarah smiled up at him.

The sound of boots scuffing dirt made them both look to the end of the garden row. Here came Levi Stoltzfus, staring at both of them.

"Matthew, what are you doing with my daughter in the garden?" His tone was low and sharp.

4

Sarah didn't mean to flinch at her father's words, but she did. "Daed, Matthew is helping me gather vegetables. Katelynn is at the stand and I needed to pick a few more things for the day, before it gets too hot."

"I see." Her Daed glanced from her to Matthew, then back to her again. "Well, best not be wasting time in idle chatter."

"Best not, jah. Matthew, thank you for your help." Sarah's cheeks flamed, and it wasn't because of the humidity. She wrested the handcart's handle from Matthew and stepped past her Daed.

It was true. She needed to focus on the here and now, not some flight of fancy to a faraway place like Florida she would never visit.

Sarah left the two men behind her and pulled the cart toward the driveway. The cart jostled along as she tugged it with a little more force than necessary. Katelynn had already unloaded the remainder of her produce, tagging her baskets for sale as she did so.

Katelynn frowned at Sarah as she approached. "Are you all right? Your face looks like one of the tomatoes. Do you need some water? I brought my little cooler." She pointed at a small square plastic box nestled between a pair of folding chairs inside the stand.

"Yes, I would like some water, thank you." Sarah wiped the perspiration from her brow. Beneath her Kapp, her scalp itched.

She paused long enough to take a few sips from a brand-new bottle of water that Katelynn handed her, before she removed the bounty that brimmed from the top of the handcart.

Katelynn motioned to the plump green tomatoes Sarah had just placed into small plastic baskets. "Speaking of tomatoes, I may buy some of those from you myself and take them home for supper. Steve and his parents are coming to have dinner with me and my parents to do some wedding planning tonight."

Sarah nodded. "Please, take a basket of tomatoes, or two, since you'll have a large group." Sarah picked up a basket of tomatoes.

"I couldn't. That will cut into our profits."

"Really, I don't mind. I've not planted any pumpkins yet, so this fall you can save some of yours for me for Thanksgiving pies. It all comes out even, anyway."

"It's a deal." Katelynn grinned, then inclined her head toward the road. "Look who's back."

Matthew was striding toward his buggy, his head down and his focus on the ground in front of him. He didn't say anything as he left, nor did he glance her way, and that troubled her.

What had her father said to Matthew, or what had Matthew said to her father? Something told her it hadn't been a warm conversation.

She stopped her presumptive thoughts about Matthew. The worst he had done was bring up talk of somewhere other than here, quiet Apple Creek. She'd heard about Pinecraft, the plain community in Florida but had never met anyone who'd been there. She'd always been curious about the place. There was nothing wrong with merely talking about it.

And how did Matthew's grandmother end up living in Florida, anyway, without the bishop's approval? Unless she was so elderly that nobody minded her going? Her mind brimmed with questions.

"I wonder why Matthew didn't say goodbye. He sure looks like he's in a hurry," Katelynn commented as she took a sip of water from her bottle.

"I'm not sure," Sarah said, truthfully enough. She suddenly recalled seeing the damage to the cashbox. "Oh, I intended to tell you as soon as you arrived, but with both Keith and Matthew here, and then me going off to pick from the garden, I forgot." She paused, taking a deep breath as she did so.

"What is it?" Katelynn's eyebrows rose.

"I think someone might have tried to pry open our cashbox. I have last night's money in my pocket—but it appears as though the box has been struck with something, to try to break the lock."

"What?" Katelynn set her baskets of tomatoes on the cooler. "Who would do such a thing?"

Sarah inclined her head toward the shelf where the cashbox sat. "Check it out," she said.

Katelynn studied the box and tested the padlock, giving it a solid tug.

"You're right. These are new marks. The duller wear-and-tear type scuffs are older." Katelynn frowned. "I know we empty the box every morning, but still . . ."

"If someone wants vegetables, they take them, and I believe in our honor system. It's worked until now." Sarah sighed. "But trying to steal the money? I don't like that. Not at all."

"I don't either." Katelynn's frown deepened. A breeze swirled around them, lifting the ends of her hair. "Should we try something different? Stop selling the extra produce altogether at night, and take the cashbox out?"

"I'm not sure. There's really no way for me to watch the stand from the house, just in case anyone comes by when we're closed."

Katelynn drummed her fingers on her chin. "We could get solar-powered digital security cameras. They are motion activated, and we could see if someone has been tampering with the box."

"That sounds expensive, especially considering we empty the box before we leave for the day, and there aren't that many after-hours customers." Sarah considered it a bit more. "I don't think I'd like to do that, not right now."

Katelynn nodded. "Well, we can try giving away the vegetables that won't keep before we close. Or we could get another cashbox with a stronger lock."

"I don't mind giving away extra vegetables." Sarah thought of the Millers. "I planned already to give some of the leftovers to Matthew and his uncle."

"I don't mind doing that, either, if it helps your neighbors." Katelynn smiled. "But do we continue to use the honor system? If the Millers don't need all the vegetables, we can still put some out for our customers."

Sarah considered the idea. "Let's keep on with what we've been doing. Up until now, everyone has been honest and has paid for the vegetables they've taken. But can you find a box with a better lock? We can also find out how to secure it better, to make tampering less appealing."

Katelynn snapped her fingers. "I've got an idea. Maybe we can cut a slot in the side of the stand and attach a box to the inside. Then people can just put their money through the slot in the stand. Then when we close up the shed at night, a thief would have a lot more trouble breaking into the stand than breaking open the box itself."

"Like a slot for mail. And we'll get a stronger box too. I don't know why we didn't think of that before."

The rumble of an engine put their conversation to a stop, for which Sarah was thankful. She didn't like thinking about a thief coming around. At least for now, they had a solution. Whether it would work, time would tell.

A man and a woman—husband and wife, Sarah presumed—got

out of the car that the man had just parked by the stand. They were followed by a tumble of children of varying ages.

"Good morning," the man called out. "Just seeing what y'all have available."

"A little bit of everything," Katelynn said. "Was there something special you were looking for? Everything we have out was fresh picked this morning."

"I'm looking for Amish jams and jellies, and soap." The mother scanned the shelves, seemingly oblivious to the children racing around and through the stand, picking up vegetables as they did so. Sarah hoped none of them would bruise the produce.

"The jams are blackberry and strawberry," Sarah said. "I'll have more apple butter after the apples ripen if you come back in a few weeks. But we don't have any soap for sale."

She watched as the oldest boy conked his brother over the head with a zucchini. Katelynn looked at Sarah, her eyebrows shooting to the top of her forehead once again.

"Boys! Mind yourselves." The mother snatched the zucchini away from her son. "Hmm, the jams look good. I'll get a jar of each, but I'm not sure if these prices are better than the other stands."

"Who's running this place, you or the Amish girl?" The man glanced from Katelynn to Sarah.

"Both of us," Sarah said. She put the woman's jars in a paper bag and accepted her money.

"I want two baskets of the green tomatoes too." The woman's jaw dropped. "Four dollars each? That's ridiculous. Never mind. Forget the whole thing. We'll go to the other stand."

"C'mon, kids, let's go," her husband said, waving his arms in the direction of their vehicle. "Honey, next time we stop, we're buying. All this in and out, in and out . . ."

The woman marched off beside her husband, muttering, and Sarah couldn't quite make out the words.

Ach, but people were harsh sometimes. Sarah and Katelynn watched as the family clambered back into their car and headed off down the road.

Katelynn huffed a breath and shook her head. "And *that* is one of the reasons dealing with the public can be so hard. I mean, really? All that fuss over green tomatoes? She'd pay the same price—or more—in a store and wouldn't be sure how fresh the produce is."

"We human beings are prone to being fickle, aren't we?" Sarah retrieved the fallen zucchini from the ground. The vegetable had a crack running end to end. "Well, looks like I'll be making zucchini bread this evening."

Idly—or perhaps not so idly—she wondered if Matthew liked zucchini bread.

Matthew stopped at McFadden's General Store, the place in Apple Creek where the locals, both Amish and English alike, picked up everything from batteries to a quick gallon of milk instead of venturing to the superstore in Savannah.

Although he liked the convenience of the store nearby, he still thought the English milk didn't taste nearly as good as the milk that came from Amish cows.

Abraham had come home from the doctor with a relatively good bill of health, and the dizzy spell he'd suffered was thought to be due to low blood sugar from not having eaten enough that day.

When Abraham realized Matthew was going to the store that

morning to pick up more nails, Abraham insisted that Matthew purchase some bags of wrapped candy—particularly anything with chocolate.

"The English doctor said I could have a piece of candy if I think I'm getting dizzy, so that's what I'll do," Abraham told him. "It'll taste a world better than taking a spoonful of Smyth's Health Elixir every morning before breakfast."

During the time since Matthew had been living with Abraham, he'd swiftly learned the value of not arguing with his uncle, who was also one of his elders. The man dug in with his opinions worse than a donkey dug in his hooves.

Outside the general store, Matthew jumped down from the buggy, then tied the horse's reins to one of the hitching posts located on the side of the building a safe distance from vehicles.

"Matthew, good to see you out and about," called out Herbert Byler, who sat across from an English man as they played a game of checkers on the porch. Herbert had been present for Matthew's meeting with the bishop and the elders the first evening Matthew had arrived in Apple Creek.

"Danke, and good morning to you," Matthew replied. He took the general store's two low steps and paused next to the two older men.

Herbert looked up at Matthew. "And how is Abraham? I understand he is home again."

"Yes, he insisted he come home this morning. He seems well enough and is ready to get back to work, or so he tells me."

The older man stroked his white beard, which nearly fell to his chest. "That's true enough. I can't see Abraham sitting in a chair in the corner for long. He's a good man, and I've known him for years. A bit stubborn, I'd say."

Matthew had to smile at Herbert's assessment. Stubborn was a good word to describe his uncle.

The older man's blue eyes filled with concern. "I pray his pride is not his undoing." Then he glanced down at the checkers in front of him, his expression changing to one of glee as he used his red checker to hop two of his opponent's black pieces.

"Well, I'll be there to help him as much as I can," Matthew said.

"Thank you for taking care of my friend, even if he doesn't see the need." Herbert paused while his opponent captured one of his red checkers.

"He's family," Matthew firmly stated.

Herbert cleared his throat. "From what I hear, there's to be an appraisal of Abraham's property. The farm and the buildings."

"An appraisal?" Why didn't he know about this?

"Yes, to put the property up for sale. You didn't know?"

Matthew shook his head. He wasn't sure how much Herbert knew about the family discussions, but evidently he knew a lot more than Matthew realized or knew himself.

"Jah. Abraham's called for it, in the event he decides to sell it outside the family. Not that he seems to relish the idea of selling, either way."

Outside the family? Something squeezed inside him.

"Abraham didn't say anything to me about that." No one had.

"Well, if the property does sell to someone other than a Miller, I hope it is sold to a plain family. We've been working to build our community here," Herbert said.

Matthew nodded. He was finding it difficult to do much besides move his head, let alone speak. He didn't realize until now how much he wanted to keep the land in the Miller family. Yet, he didn't have enough of his own money to do that. He could make a down payment, but if he was joining this district, officially, he would not be getting a loan from a bank to buy the property. It wasn't their way.

Matthew spoke again, at last. "I'd like to purchase the property myself, if Abraham decides he must sell it." Matthew had to think his uncle would want the land to stay in the family.

"Well, perhaps you can, somehow." Herbert rubbed his hands together. It appeared as if the man's attention had drifted back fully to the game in front of him, now that his opponent had stacked up more of Herbert's red checkers.

Matthew entered the general store, his thoughts troubled and jangling as harshly as the bell over the door. His head still reeled from the brief conversation he'd had with Levi Stoltzfus earlier.

It hadn't been specifically about Sarah, but more about his place in the community and for him to watch his actions very carefully.

Matthew picked up the needed nails and even a small carton of chocolate milk that he could drink on the way home.

In many ways, he was still learning the nuances of the community he was trying to join. Wolfesboro had its own ways and practices, which kept it separate enough from the larger, English community around it. But he had begun to learn that Apple Creek was its own animal.

Matthew stepped into the narrow aisle that had candy, potato chips, and other treats on display and picked up a couple of bags of candy.

"You got a sweet tooth?" a young, female voice said at his elbow.

Matthew almost jumped at the sound of the voice, he'd been so lost in thought.

He glanced at the speaker, a woman in her early twenties who wore a white tank top and denim cutoff shorts, with frayed strands that hung in wisps on her tan legs. Her coy smile gave an invitation to linger in the aisle and chat.

During his Rumspringa days, this young woman would be the kind he might want to take on a date and get to know better. She was certainly pretty. But those days were firmly behind him.

"I don't have much of a sweet tooth, but my uncle does. He's sixty-eight, just got out of the hospital, and wants candy." Matthew held up the bags of wrapped chocolate drops. "So, he'll get candy. Have a nice day."

"You have a nice day too." She grinned at him.

He gave her a nod before heading for the cashier. He was uncomfortable with some of the English now, and uncomfortable with some of his own plain people. He wondered, not for the first time, if it really was possible to go home again.

5

Sarah's back ached from sitting on the wooden bench. Her eyelids drooped and she struggled to keep her focus on Bishop's message Sunday morning.

It was a good message too, about keeping pure before God in the midst of a world full of distractions.

Her best friend, Lydia Fry, gave her a firm jab in the ribs. "You snorted," she whispered.

"Did not." But Sarah cleared her throat anyway. She shifted on the bench into a more comfortable position.

Her Mamm gave both of them a glance from where she sat on the bench in front of them. No, they weren't *Kinner* anymore, but Sarah supposed a mother might always think of her daughter as a child, no matter how old she was. A young woman—Ida Lapp—sat beside Mamm and held a young child who slept blissfully on Ida's shoulder.

Finally it was time to stand for the ending prayer, which could go on for five minutes or more, depending on the elder doing the praying. After that would come announcements, and then they would all take part of the delicious spread to be laid out on tables that stretched the length of the farmyard.

"Talk about distractions." Lydia gave Sarah another nudge. "The new man, Matthew. He lives right next door to you."

"Jah," Sarah whispered. "We've spoken several times." But not since yesterday morning at the farm stand. It was just as well, anyway, especially given Bishop's message.

Herbert Byler began the closing prayer and Lydia kept silent. But Sarah—who struggled to fix her attention to Herbert's words—found herself anticipating Lydia's response to her comment after the final "Amen" had been uttered.

She did pray to be undistracted by the world around her and to keep her focus on the Amish ways. They lived simply for a reason, to remain close to God and be fit for an eternal reward, God willing.

But what if the distraction wasn't out in "the world" but was standing with the other men of the district, elbow to elbow, across the rows of backless wooden benches from her?

"Amen," she murmured with the rest of them.

An announcement then came, a reminder of the young people's singing next Saturday evening, at the home of Bishop and Louisa Hilty. Louisa, Sarah reflected, was particularly fond of singing and also enjoyed filling their home with the younger people of the community. She hoped when she was Louisa's age she could host singings too.

"You should try to make sure that Matthew is at the singing," Lydia stated matter-of-factly as soon as announcements were over and conversations began to swirl around them.

"Why would I do that?" Sarah didn't even know if the man could sing or liked to sing.

"Because, if you have spoken several times and he has been here but a week, clearly he has an interest in you." Lydia shook her head, as if Sarah was being particularly dense. "Anyway, I am going to the singing with Thad Graber, so we can all go together in an even number if you are there with Matthew."

At that, Sarah chuckled. "It sounds as though you have things already planned."

"Well, all I'd have to do is mention it to Thad, and he can ask Matthew to come with us, if you're shy about suggesting he come too."

Sarah's cheeks flamed as she glanced around. "No, I'm not shy about asking him if he plans to go. It's just . . . I don't think it's a good idea."

Lydia fell silent, and the two made their way to where the women had started placing out dishes for the massive supper on tables laid end to end beneath a large oak tree in the Hiltys' yard. The men were already lining up, ready to eat what the women had prepared.

"Well," Lydia said, folding her arms in front of her, "I don't see why it's not a good idea."

"Because he's not been baptized, nor proven yet."

"Like that has stopped you two from talking."

Sarah shrugged. "If Matthew comes to the singing, then he comes." She took a deep breath, hoping her words sounded nonchalant. She certainly didn't feel that way. "We should grab some dishes and pitch in, instead of standing here."

Anything to stop the talk about Matthew, who, she realized, was now staring at her from where he stood talking with several of the men in line.

Sarah took another deep breath. A light breeze blew as she made her way under the shade of the tree, which would provide welcome coolness compared to inside the house. Chatter flowed around them of friends and neighbors catching up on the latest news. This was the best part of being plain, Sarah reflected. On days like today, she felt the warmth of community and knew exactly where she belonged in the world. Apple Creek, she knew, would always be home to her.

Sarah and Lydia followed a trail of women into the kitchen, where an assortment of dishes, platters, and storage containers had been stacked until the meeting was over. Beside the back door, outside, a refrigerator sat, looking a bit out of place but powered with a generator to keep food cold during the meeting.

"Ah, here, Sarah." Mrs. Hilty handed Sarah a wrapped loaf, along with a cutting board and a knife. "If you could, bring this out along with that basket on the table and slice the bread. That sourdough is my husband's favorite, so it won't do to run out."

"Yes, glad to, Mrs. Hilty." She picked up the basket and held it steady while the bishop's wife deposited a loaf, a cutting board, and a knife.

Sarah stepped outside and found an empty spot at the food table where she could slice the bread. Lydia popped up to the table and stood beside her.

Sarah decided to pepper Lydia with questions of her own before Lydia could start asking again about Matthew.

"So, you said you are going to the singing with Thad Graber? You never told me you'd started speaking to him. Are you courting and you didn't tell me?"

"Well, it happened two weeks ago, after last meeting. Thad asked me if he could escort me home after the singing. We may be courting, soon enough." Lydia's cheeks flushed as she fiddled with the spoon sticking into a mound of steaming mashed potatoes on the table in front of her.

Thad Graber was a good-looking, hardworking young man who built handcrafted furniture and aspired to open a store in Apple Creek. Lydia had been quite taken with him for some time.

"I see." Sarah deliberately used a teasing tone.

"We've known each other practically our entire lives, and we are both planning to stay here in Apple Creek." Lydia grinned. "My Mamm made me promise that I wouldn't marry someone who might take me away from here."

"That would be a good promise to keep." The community would grow naturally, so long as its young people would marry and stay here, instead of heading to a larger community. And if new people moved here, of course. Her thoughts turned to her sister. "I didn't tell you yet, but Emma and Jacob might be moving back."

"To Apple Creek?" Lydia touched Sarah's elbow. "When?"

"Sometime this fall, maybe." She realized she probably shouldn't mention anything about the property purchase. Nothing was settled, and the move might not happen. In fact, her father had said nothing more about it since the other night.

"I still can't believe Jacob switched from you to her, faster than a bee heading to another flower." Lydia's brow furrowed.

Sarah finished slicing the loaf of bread and picked up the crumb-covered cutting board. She sprinkled the crumbs on the grass.

"That was a long time ago, and both Emma and he are happy." Sarah glanced across the yard. Now Matthew and several other men were busily loading the benches used for church services into a space inside the Hiltys' barn. The benches would be moved to the next home to host the meeting, two Sundays from now.

Lydia sighed. "You're right, they're happy. But I don't like my best friend being hurt, all teasing aside. Anyway, you do need to join us at the singing because it will be fun, and I'm ready for a night of fun after this summer of work, work, work. If I have to can one more jar of green beans, I'll scream."

At that, Sarah laughed. "But you'll love eating them this winter."

Mrs. Hilty approached them. "Thank you for your help. Sarah, will you be holding a quilting day on Wednesday? I should have reminded the Bishop to announce it, but I forgot about it myself until just now."

"Yes, I am still planning to quilt on Wednesday. We'll start at nine o'clock, or as soon as everyone gets there. I'll welcome help. Mamm and I will also make sandwiches and lemonade." Sarah had almost forgotten about it herself.

"Good, I look forward to it. We're going to have the most beautiful quilt at the Haiti auction this year." The woman beamed.

Sarah did too, at the words that would sound so prideful if coming from anyone else. "We're going to do our best. I'm very grateful to you all for your help with the pattern. I knew it was more than I would be able to do on my own, and more than I would have time for."

"I was glad to help. I'm looking forward to seeing you then." Mrs. Hilty moved along to a cluster of women, all talking and wiping their hands on dishcloths.

"I could see you as a bishop's wife, one day," Lydia said. "You always seem to know the right thing to say. Me, I'd be letting the words out faster than a chicken running from the coop."

Sarah shook her head. "I don't think I want to be a bishop's wife. I wouldn't want people watching me, waiting for me to say the *wrong* thing."

The men were already eating, and Lydia disappeared, presumably to load up her plate so she could find a spot close enough to Thad Graber so she could at least see him during the meal.

Sarah found herself looking across the tables at Matthew Miller, who was seated with her father.

She could only hope their conversation would be civil.

Matthew had taken one of the last spots at the series of tables lined up end to end in the Hiltys' immense yard. His stomach growled as he sat down with his brimming plate, which bore an assortment of home-cooked goodness, including hearty meat loaf, creamy potatoes, and green beans seasoned with bacon and onions. His stomach growled again.

Neither he nor Abraham could manage cooking more than the basics. Their meals at home were definitely not like this.

Prior to the meal, Mrs. Hilty had told Abraham that she would send the two of them home with plenty of leftovers that would last several days, if they kept the food on ice, which he would certainly do. Abraham had an ancient icebox from older days which he still insisted upon using rather than buying a small refrigerator and a generator.

Matthew took a bite of the meat loaf. It was moist and delicious. The mashed potatoes were a perfect complement, loaded with melted cheddar and sour cream. It was a hot day for such heavy food, but he didn't care. He tried not to meet Sarah's brown, expressive gaze from a few yards away.

He didn't succeed. Their glances lingered, and her cheeks shot full of color before she cast a glance down.

"Isn't that right, Sarah?" he heard Mrs. Stoltzfus saying. "What do you think?"

Sarah nodded, but her expression told him she wasn't quite sure what her mother had asked.

"So, a blue binding or black binding on the quilt?" Mrs. Stoltzfus asked as they headed to the ladies' table.

"Blue, dark blue," Sarah replied. She did not look his way.

"Matthew, it is good to see Abraham here today with you." Levi brought Matthew's attention back to the table.

Matthew saw his uncle in the process of devouring the food on his plate a few seats down from them. "Yes, he's very glad to be here."

He prepared himself for whatever comments or questions might come next.

"Some of us will play cornhole after we eat. We're going to form some teams. You can join us, if you would like to," said Levi.

"Thank you, I believe I will," Matthew said. "As long as Abraham would like to stay, I'll stay and visit too."

He knew being out and about would be good for his uncle, who seemed sprier after the last incident. His appetite was certainly good.

Matthew picked up a buttered biscuit, using it to swipe up some of the delicious sauce that accompanied the meat loaf. So far, so good.

If he visited with the rest of the men, it would remove him from the source of his present distraction. *Sarah.*

"We will be there, Friday after next, to help repair your roof," Levi continued. "It is too much for one man to do, with everything else required of a farm. We should be finished in one day, along with any other repairs needed on the property. I know you are still getting used to everything that needs to be done on a farm."

Matthew nodded. "It's true, and I—we—thank you for the help. I have ordered the materials, and they'll be delivered in plenty of time." Matthew also appreciated that Bishop Hilty had announced that the Millers needed help with repairs to the barn, and that they would meet at the farm, shortly after daybreak.

"You ready to swing a hammer, then?"

Matthew nodded. "I've done a bit of roofing over the years myself. It's hard work, but satisfying. And with enough hands, we can get it done quickly, like you said."

Another man, seated beside Levi, spoke up. "I hear you were out with the English for a long time. Did you ever use one of those electric nail guns? I'll bet those make work go good and fast."

"That they do, for sure," Matthew replied. "I've used one for many projects. Cabinets, furniture, and for building sheds and other things. It saves a body's energy too. A man's arm and shoulder can ache after swinging a hammer hundreds of times or more. Not that I need to tell you all that," he added, realizing how English he sounded.

"Humph." Levi shook his head. "It doesn't hurt for a man to use the muscles God gave him. No shame in hard work, as we are commanded to work in the Scriptures."

Matthew didn't take the bait. It wasn't always well-defined among them, what was considered laziness and what was considered being efficient. The answer depended on who you asked.

He had never minded using power tools to get a job done more quickly and sometimes with better quality, although that had a lot to do with how a tool was used. But the handcrafted wooden furniture of the Amish people was always the best, in his opinion.

Aloud, Matthew said, "But then, I also believe that handcrafted and handmade are better built than something made with the help of a machine."

He realized he was still getting used to speaking German again. He hadn't forgotten it altogether, but since he hadn't spoken it regularly for years, he sometimes faltered.

Matthew took his empty plate and left the table. He allowed himself another look at Sarah. Her smile, her rich brown eyes glowing as she talked with the others around her, almost made him pause to stare.

He mentally nudged himself to pay attention to where he was. It would be a long time before he could prove himself to the district. They'd accepted him in a preliminary sort of way, a "let's see how he does" approach to the wanderer who had come back to his people.

Wolfesboro was a much larger community, true, but there he had felt even more under the thumb and watchful eyes of the leadership. They didn't even allow the bright-orange safety triangles on buggies there, but here in Apple Creek, the bishop and elders encouraged it for the safety of their people as they traveled poorly lit back roads in the evenings.

Ach, but there he was, passing judgment on the other ones in

Wolfesboro, and he had promised himself he wouldn't be one to do that. His father, mother, and most of his family still lived there, and he loved them. He just couldn't live with them.

It was an unspoken truth held between him and his parents that they didn't think he would be accepted in Wolfesboro, that it was too strict for him and he had too much history there. He wanted Apple Creek to be better.

So far, he'd found it was. He was building a tenuous footing in his new community, one he planned to strengthen the more he was here.

Matthew handed his plate to a woman, who placed it into a bucket along with other dirty plates.

"Matthew, it's time for cornhole. Come join your pair!" a male voice called across the yard, where men had begun to gather.

He thanked the woman for helping him with the plate, then strolled across to join the men, who had begun to pair off for a cornhole tournament. He removed his hat and let the breeze blow through his hair for just a moment, blessedly cool on his scalp.

Levi Stoltzfus stepped away from him; the motion wasn't lost on Matthew. Levi had been more or less civil to him at the table, but ever since the conversation at the garden, when Levi had seen him walking with Sarah, there'd been an unspoken warning: Sarah was off-limits and there would be little that Matthew could do to prove himself worthy to call on her, even though Sarah was plenty old enough to choose for herself.

He headed for Herbert Byler, who was snapping his suspenders as he talked to his checkers rival, Homer Chupp. "Herbert, need a partner? I'm a fairly good thrower."

The older man eyed him. "Well, I guess we'll see about that, won't we? You can be sure for all the cautions against pride, we shall see plenty of it today, depending on who wins. And who doesn't."

Homer and Levi counted the paces between the two cornhole boxes before the teams of men drew straws to see who would go first.

There were four teams, with Levi and another man competing, as well as Thad Graber matched up with Abraham.

Thad Graber, a few years younger than Matthew, talked about the furniture shop he wanted to open come spring, if all went well.

"I found an empty storefront in downtown Apple Creek that I can lease," Thad told them as they started the game. "Once I fix it up, I can stock it with furniture."

"There's always a demand for *gut* furniture," observed Herbert as he and Matthew stood at one end of the setup, and Levi and his partner at the other.

"But in town among the English?" Levi sounded skeptical. "Better to set up at your farm, or I should say, your Daed's farm. People will find you." He eyed the hole in the box near Matthew and Herbert and tossed his beanbag. It slid to a stop on the surface of the box but didn't make it into the hole.

Matthew watched as Levi tossed his next beanbag. This one made it into the hole and Levi looked triumphant.

"I think it will be easier for customers to find my shop in town," said Thad. "My Daed won't want a lot of traffic going by the house, and up and down the driveway. Too much noise."

"Ach, he's got a point there," Herbert said.

Levi shrugged. "Jah, I suppose. But it's good to see that you, one of our younger men, are planning to stay here in Apple Creek and be a productive member of the community."

The glance Levi gave Matthew spoke volumes.

He doesn't trust me. Matthew wanted to fix that. He wanted Levi to trust him. He wanted *all* of them to trust him.

6

On Wednesday morning, two horse-drawn buggies had made muddy tracks in the driveway and three sets of footprints made a trail up the steps and onto the porch of the Stoltzfus farmhouse.

The screen door let cooler air rush through the living room, where Sarah, her mother, and three other ladies from the district sat around a quilting frame that filled the modest space.

Thunder, lightning, and strong rains before dawn had woken Sarah from a sound sleep, and she wondered how many would show up to work on the quilt that day.

Lydia had braved the storm. At least there was someone around her own age there who wasn't already tending babies.

The other ladies were Patience and Charity Oberholtz, who knew everything about everyone in Apple Creek and were most happy to share the latest news, even though it had only been a few days since the district's Sunday gathering at the Hiltys'.

Patience, mother of six and grandmother of eight—so far—lamented that her other daughter had been gone from Apple Creek for two months.

"I miss her terribly, but she and Peter are very happy in Wolfesboro." Patience looked over the nose of her glasses as she studied the quilt block directly in front of her.

"Jah," said Sarah's mother, "I can scarcely believe I have not seen Emma since Christmas. I hope, though, that they will return to Apple Creek very soon."

"What will they do? Will they be living with you?" Patience asked.

Sarah didn't miss Lydia's quick sideways glance in her direction. "They will, at first. Because of the baby. But if all goes well, Jacob will have his own farm, close by."

At that moment, Sarah's quilting needle slipped and poked the side of her thumb beneath the sandwiched layers of fabric and batting. She winced, letting out a yelp as she did so.

Mamm jumped at the sudden noise. "Ach, Sarah. Take care with the needle."

Sarah pulled her hand from beneath the fabric. A tiny drop of blood bloomed on her thumb. "Best I clean this up so not to spoil the quilt."

"I'll help." Lydia stood.

Sarah strode from the living room to the kitchen to rinse her finger and dry it. It was one thing for Emma and Jacob to move back, but to *live* with them in the same house? She hadn't allowed herself to think about where they would live, but of course it would be here. Would it be uncomfortable? Would she feel like a fool? *Do I still love Jacob?*

She rubbed at her thumb with a little more vigor than necessary. She paused. No. She didn't love Jacob anymore. But it had hurt horribly, when he rejected her with no explanation. She'd let herself be vulnerable and let herself care for him, believing that he felt the same way about her.

Then, inexplicably, he'd pulled away from her just when she thought he might be speaking to her father to formally ask to court and eventually marry her. But those conversations had been about Emma. And the closeness between her sister, her once-dearest friend, was never the same after that. Perhaps Emma felt self-conscious or guilty at her feelings for Jacob when she knew Sarah had liked him first.

But Jacob did have winsome ways and could make someone laugh easily. He could speak well, and the stories he wrote about the Amish life were beautiful. A few of his pieces had even been included in *The Budget* newspaper. He had been the smartest one in school, Sarah recalled from long ago.

"Are you all right?" Lydia whispered behind her. "I know it's just a simple needle poke. We've done that hundreds of times."

"Jah, we have." She glanced at her sore thumb.

"But you didn't know Emma and Jacob would be moving in with you when, or if—when—they move back here."

"No. I didn't think about that at all."

"Maybe things are not so pleasant for them in Wolfesboro, so that makes being here in Apple Creek more appealing," Lydia mused.

"Maybe." Sarah didn't mention the baby. She'd missed her sister, but the distance had also allowed her to ignore the other gap between them because of Jacob. "Maybe my sister and I will be closer again, and not just because we will be under the same roof. That will be a *gut* thing."

"Sarah? Lydia?" Mamm called out from the living room.

"Coming, Mamm." Sarah tossed the dishcloth into a bucket and returned to the living room.

She and Lydia took their places, side by side, at the quilt frame once again.

Sarah found the offending needle and this time she attempted to stitch more carefully, no matter what anyone brought up in the course of conversation.

"I wonder if we'll be able to put in one more quilt before the auction," Sarah said aloud. "Although, it feels like this quilt has taken much longer than usual to complete."

"Well," said Patience, "if we gathered together to quilt more frequently, then certainly we could."

Sarah didn't miss Lydia's eye roll.

"I wonder if the ladies of Sunnyside Church in Florida will donate more than one quilt," Charity said. "If we do another, then we can raise more money."

Sarah studied the quilt's design. It was called Light in the Valley, with a series of curved blocks changing in color from light pink, to indigo, and then to almost white in the center. She'd purchased all the fabric herself with money from her garden produce and was thankful she could do so. For that reason, she'd chosen the design, and her mother had helped her cut the pieces and sew them together to form the top.

"Ow." Lydia pulled the needle from the fabric. "Seems my needle has its own will today too, ignoring the thimble."

At that, Sarah chuckled, although the other women did not.

"Jah, I think if we could start another quilt right after this one, we can ship it the same time," Mamm said.

"We could always make a scrap quilt too," Patience observed. "It might not sell for as much at auction as one of the more elaborate designs, so maybe we could just sell it here in Apple Creek and donate the money to the school."

"I would love to go to that auction in Florida, someday, even this coming January," Sarah said. "It would be quite a sight to see. All the plain people, from so many places, all in one place."

"Oh, that would be a sight, now, wouldn't it?" Patience smiled. "It's not unheard of. But you know it would be an expense to travel there, then to secure accommodations. I read in *The Budget* that a brand-new hotel is almost built. That's got to be expensive."

"Have you ever been to Pinecraft?" Sarah asked. "The beach and the ocean, so close by . . ."

Patience nodded. "Once, when I was much younger. We went to visit my grandparents who owned a small house there. We filled up the place, wall to wall. The volleyball games, the singings and suppers, games in the park . . ."

"But it's idleness." Mamm sighed. "I see nothing wrong with spending an afternoon or an evening playing games or singing. But to do so for days on end? I would feel guilty. And then, there's the money spent to get there in the first place."

"I still think it would be lovely to go." Sarah decided not to voice that she'd already started putting a bit of savings by for the trip. She hadn't told anyone.

Charity looked up from her stitching. "Well, don't speak that too loudly. Bishop might hear you." She chuckled.

"Now, Charity, it is not that bad." Patience shook her head. "We can speak of things like amusements and such."

"The way he talks about idleness and distractions sometimes, I wonder." Charity looked down again and began stitching.

"It's for our best," Mamm said. "Keeping things simple keeps us close to Gött. Our lives are for His service and for others."

Sarah nodded. "I wonder what the Amish church is like in Sarasota."

"I am sure it is quite different from ours," Mamm said.

"I can only remember what it was like from when I was younger." Patience tied off the end of her thread and freed her needle. "Black and white on Sundays, with straw hats for the men. White sheer Kapps for the women. Dark aprons. Not so different, in some ways."

"Yes, but all that electricity . . ." Mamm commented.

"I wonder if they have air-conditioning and if they use electricity all the time," Sarah said. "I'll say it as loudly as I want, there are some days I wish we had air-conditioning."

"Ah, that is the truth." Charity nodded. "Well, fall is coming soon enough, and then we'll be longing for the sun's warmth. Best we enjoy it now while we can."

The women fell silent and continued to stitch away.

Surely, Sarah thought, she could save up some money and hire a driver to take her. Perhaps the same one who drove Matthew's own grandmother to Florida, like he had suggested. As far as a place to stay, she could figure that out too. Sarah determined, the next time she spoke to Matthew, she would ask him more about the Amish community by the beach.

Matthew gazed out at the rain-soaked fields, the leaves of the soybean plants weighed down with water. Today was a day to see to indoor work and possibly replace some boards in the horse stalls.

"Women's work. I can't stand it," Abraham muttered from where he sat on the porch. "Should have married again when I had the chance, if but to have clean clothes whenever I need them. What was I thinking?"

A steel washtub full of laundry and a washboard rested on the porch floor in front of him, and Abraham slid one of his work shirts up and down to scrub it clean in the sudsy water.

Matthew tried not to grin at the older man's complaint. Yes, it was one thing to be a bachelor in an Amish community, but to be so for as long as Abraham had, it was an oddity indeed. No wonder the family was in a pickle on what to do about him.

"So, did you have the chance, once, to remarry?"

"Jah, I did. Lois Schrock. She was the prettiest young lady at the singing, with a kind heart."

"What happened?" Matthew had never heard the story before. He had only seen Abraham a few times while growing up in Wolfesboro. Until now, his uncle hadn't spoken of his younger years.

"I was too shy. I didn't have the nerve to speak to her, not about my intentions, that is. We walked to singings together. Well, walked with our friends. Then I lost my chance. She went on to marry someone else. And before that, I only had five years with my Joanna." Abraham scrubbed harder.

"That's too bad."

"It wasn't the will of Gött for me. I accept it." Abraham shrugged. "Still, I could be having someone else do my laundry while I see to other things around here."

"When this rain lets up, I'll check on some repairs to be made inside the barn. I can't cut hay today."

"The horses are happy for the break too, I think." Abraham nodded in the direction of the barn. He continued scrubbing clothes in the washtub.

Matthew wondered about the wisdom of washing clothes on a rainy day. Instead of using the clothesline outside, Abraham would have to hang up the freshly washed clothing around the house, most of it probably in the kitchen. The clothing would take many hours to dry and then Abraham would likely grumble about not wanting to wait until the return of sunny days when he could hang everything outside.

However, Matthew knew better than to try to argue with Abraham about something once the man had his mind made up. No wonder the family had given up on getting him to move out of the farmhouse—for the moment.

Well, Matthew decided he wasn't going to try to talk the man out of his home, not if the ones who knew him best couldn't convince him already.

"Will you be planting a winter wheat crop?" Matthew asked, settling on a safer topic of conversation.

Abraham wrung out a shirt, letting the water spill onto the porch floor. "No, I don't believe so. I'm tired. No need for a cover crop, either. I'll let the fields rest until spring."

"What will be ready for harvest next?" He rarely had the opportunity to ask Abraham about his plans for the farm or what was to come. In the short time Matthew had been here, Abraham had not informed Matthew about his plans or intentions.

Abraham grunted, wringing out another shirt as he did so and setting the damp cloth over the back of a wooden chair. "You're full of questions today. At least you're not asking me what I will do with this place."

"I'd like to know what you plan to do, I admit, so I can be the best help I can be. I helped my Daed on our land long ago. Can't say as I've done much farming the last few years, but it has all come back to me, the longer I've been here." Matthew tugged on one of his suspenders.

"You are more of a woodworker than one who works the land. You build things."

"I do. But if I can help my family by farming, if that's Gött's will for me, I will gladly do it."

Abraham stopped scrubbing and eyed Matthew intently. "Gött has a different way for each of us. Do you think your way is here, on this farm?"

"For now, yes," Matthew admitted. "I know you need the help, and the family is concerned about you."

"They all want to see what I will do with the land is what it is. I know my hiring someone for an appraisal confused them." His uncle shrugged. "Your own Daed probably wants you to have the property."

Matthew decided to risk voicing his idea. "I could buy it from you. I don't have much saved, nowhere near what this land might be worth in an English sale. Maybe my Daed would help me. I don't know."

He'd never spoken aloud of any of the ideas, which up to now had only been a dream.

Abraham nodded, slowly. He leaned over, resting his elbow on one knee. "What I am about to tell you, I have told no one. Yes, this will likely be my last harvest."

"But you said you'd let the land rest until spring." Where was his uncle going with this?

"Jah, I know. But it is time. I haven't said anything because I won't move to a Daedi Haus in Wolfesboro. Or move in with my brother."

"But where would you go?"

"Florida. I hear from my mother about the life there, in Pinecraft. I would not have to wash my clothes by hand. I can go to the laundry there. I can walk to the market for food that I can heat in a microwave oven. I can do many things I cannot do here, without questions from the bishop."

Matthew well understood that feeling. Living as Old Order was not for everyone, even if generators or battery-operated items were permitted. He thought he'd seen an Amish man with a cell phone one day at the general store but hadn't been certain because the man caught him looking and walked away briskly as he tucked the possibly contraband item into his pocket.

"You know what I mean? You've thought the same things, haven't you?" Abraham asked, at last.

"Yes, I do, and I have."

"If you buy this land, you must work it. Every season, in all the weather. You must coax it to yield and pray for God's blessings and good rains. You must have help, *gut* help, and sometimes good help is hard to find, as I have found. Until now."

But as Matthew looked out over the fields, the barn, and the other small outbuildings that held the plow and the buggy and wagon, he knew he ought to give it his best. "I must try, though, to do what I can."

Abraham grunted. "You're different than the others, from being among the English for so long. I don't know that the life here is the one for you. Could you be truly thankful, if this was all you had?"

"I would do my best to live as God wants me to, and to keep my life plain and simple here."

"Huh." Abraham went back to scrubbing some trousers. "That's not really an answer, but I'll accept it for now."

Matthew nodded. "Thank you." He stepped toward the porch. "I'm going to check the barn, see where the worst leaks are, while it's wet."

"I'll be here, doing my women's work." Abraham chuckled as Matthew took the steps from the porch.

The mud squished around the soles of Matthew's boots as he made his way across the farmyard to the barn, where the animals were tucked inside away from the rain, except for some of the cows, who stood in the drizzle now that the downpour was over from earlier in the morning.

He slid the barn door open. Without sunlight, the interior was a bit dim, and yet it was warm from the animals inside. Matthew squinted. Perhaps he should have brought a lantern as he had earlier in the morning when he went out in the downpour to milk the cow and put out feed.

What were once puddles in the early morning had turned into a small river that ran the length of the barn and to the outdoor pen. Matthew tilted his head back to look up toward the roof. Where there were shingles before, now he could see to the gray sky above. Not good at all.

A gust of wind blew through the barn, rattling the doors and the window to the hayloft.

With a cracking of wood, splintering boards rained down on him from the roof. He felt a bolt of pain to his head, white-hot light in one eye, crushing weights on his shoulders, arms, and back—

Matthew landed in the muddy water.

7

The screen door at the Stoltzfus home opened then shut with a bang. All the women flinched where they sat around the quilting frame.

They all stared as an elderly Amish man—Abraham Miller—stumbled into the living room. He managed to keep his footing, even as he leaned over and tried to catch his breath. He used the back of the nearest chair for support. Mud clung to his boots.

"Help!" Abraham gasped. "I tried to stop the bleeding, but I can't get the boards off him." The man's breath came in heaving gulps.

Sarah leaped to her feet. "What bleeding? Who's hurt?" She noticed some red stains on his hands, and on the knees of his trousers as he leaned over, bracing his hands on his knees.

"Matthew," Abraham gasped. "Boards . . . fell . . . roof in the barn. All over him. He's hurt. Blood."

Mamm stood. "My husband is in town with the buggy."

"We can go for help." Patience was already standing up, tugging Charity to her feet as she did so.

"We need to go to him. Is he awake?" Sarah choked out the words.

"Don't know . . . can't move him." As soon as Abraham spoke the words, he collapsed onto the braided rag rug. His face took on a gray, pale color.

Mamm shot to his side. "Abraham!" She tried to help the old man to a seated position, but he pushed her away, then sagged to the floor again.

"We need to get him to the doctor, quickly," said Mamm.

Despite his protests, the women helped the older man into Patience's buggy and eased him onto the back seat.

Patience climbed onto the driver's seat and they left for town.

"We'll see to Matthew." Lydia tugged on Sarah's arm.

Sarah had already slipped on a sweater to fend off the cool dampness outside. As quickly as they could, she and Lydia left the house, crossed the yard, then scooted through the fence and began to cross the Stoltzfus's cornfield between the two farms, pushing their way through the stalks. It was more direct than heading down the driveway, along the road, then to the Millers' drive.

The cornstalk leaves struck Sarah's arms and face with stinging slaps as she continued to push through, leaving Lydia behind her. Finally she was at the Millers' fence, where she slid between the rails, then continued on a muddy path through the rows of soggy soybeans.

She caught a glimpse of the open barn door and raced for that.

"Matthew!" Sarah stumbled into the dim space inside.

He groaned where he lay, surrounded by splintered boards and mud. She skittered to his side and began to lift boards off him. Lydia appeared, out of breath, and helped.

"See if you can find some clean water and rags," Sarah ordered, kneeling down beside Matthew and not caring that her favorite dress and apron were now brown and smeared with mud. They'd wash, easily enough.

Lydia raced in the direction of the farmhouse.

Matthew touched his head and winced. "Head. Hurts. Where's Abraham?" He tried to sit up.

"He came to get us. Here." Sarah took his arm, but he groaned again and lay back down. She examined the gash, which was perhaps two inches long and parallel to his hairline. Specks of wood were embedded in the cut, fresh blood oozing around them.

Lydia reappeared and held up a hand towel. "I found this inside by the washboard. It's damp, but clean."

Sarah realized with a start that she was holding one of Matthew's hands. She released it and took the cloth, which she folded, pressing the absorbent rectangle gently but firmly to Matthew's forehead.

Her heart raced. "Stay awake, try to stay awake." She couldn't remember why, but when young Otto, the bishop's grandson, had fallen off a beam during a barn raising and hit his head, someone kept telling him to stay awake as they took care of him.

Matthew blinked, studying her face as he did so. "You are kind . . . beautiful . . . so gentle."

"Hush, now." Sarah could feel Lydia's knowing look above her. Her face flamed, even though she knew his words meant nothing, the ramblings of a man with a head injury.

"Where's Abraham?" Matthew tried to shift to face the doorway, but the movement was clearly too painful to sustain.

"He came to tell us you were in trouble, and then he collapsed," Lydia said. "Patience and Charity Oberholtz are taking him for help."

"If something happens to him, because of me . . ." Matthew closed his eyes.

"We will pray nothing does. If it does, it will not be your fault." Sarah tried to keep her voice from quavering.

The sound of a buggy arriving sounded outside the barn. Mamm appeared, and Sarah drew a breath of relief. Mamm would know what to do.

"How is he? I was going to suggest you take Lydia's buggy, but you two ran off before I could speak, so I used it myself." She leaned over, then pulled back. "It seems you have done the correct thing." Sarah felt a small swell of pride, which she tamped down. It was wrong to be proud, particularly when she'd just been doing her duty.

Matthew struggled to a seated position, bringing himself closer to Sarah's eye level. "Thank you. Beware the roof. I knew it needed repair . . . didn't think it was this bad. The boards may not be done falling." He heaved a deep breath, as though he'd had to force the words from his mouth.

Sarah stood, taking a step back to allow Matthew to stand on his own. Still, she wanted to help him to the buggy. "We should get you to a doctor."

"Sarah is right," Mamm said decisively. "There could be injuries we cannot see."

"I don't need to be seen by a doctor," Matthew said. "It's only a flesh wound and not very deep. Head wounds bleed excessively."

"I'm sorry about the towel. It was very clean." Lydia motioned to the cloth bundle that Matthew held to his forehead.

Matthew glanced up. "I don't think Abraham will even notice it's gone."

Mamm motioned toward the buggy. "Lydia, Sarah, and I will ride with you to Louisa Hilty. She will inspect and care for the wound with her supplies. Likely she will need to check for other injuries as well."

"I don't think it's that bad," Matthew insisted.

Sarah shook her head. "The cut is at least two inches long. Please, it will heal better if she sees to it, I'm sure." She looked down to see her hand on his arm and quickly removed it.

"I suppose you're right." His gaze at her was warm, and Sarah diverted her eyes to the horse which stood patiently waiting for them all.

Louisa was not only the bishop's wife, but she was one of the people the district called upon for help with medical matters. Going to an English doctor was only for truly serious matters.

They all piled into the buggy, with Lydia driving and Sarah in the front seat, and Mamm taking the seat beside Matthew in the back.

Lydia maneuvered the horse to head out toward the road that led toward the Hiltys' farm. All the while, Sarah's distracted thoughts led her to remember what it had been like to hold Matthew's hand, warm and soft and strong despite the injury.

Had Mamm noticed her behavior?

From now on, Sarah suspected she'd have a hard time not noticing Matthew herself, nor the feelings that surged within her at the very thought of him.

Matthew's head throbbed. Mrs. Hilty had cleaned the wound carefully, then used some healing salve and topped it with butterfly bandages to close the gash. He hadn't wanted any fuss, and he hadn't gotten any fuss. Yet, he was glad he had given in to Sarah's insistence to seek some kind of medical care.

He now stood at the foot of Abraham's bed at the hospital closest to Apple Creek. His uncle was reclined with his head propped up with three pillows on the bed and seemed embarrassed by the attention provided to him by the medical staff, along with the members of the Amish community who had come when they heard he wasn't well again.

At the moment, it was just Matthew and his father, who had come from Wolfesboro when he had heard the news.

"I overdid it when I went to find help for you," Abraham explained. "I feel perfectly fine now. I just need a piece of candy."

"Yes, you feel perfectly fine now that you are on oxygen and lying abed." Matthew's father shook his head, crossing his arms over his chest. "We need to have a strong family conversation, because this cannot go on like it is."

"No one can force me from my home." Abraham's voice was firm.

Matthew hung back from entering the conversation. His role was to help Abraham get through the growing season and the harvest—his last one as Abraham had confirmed himself that morning. What came next for both of them was uncertain.

Matthew's Daed unfolded his arms, then began to pace the room. "No one is forcing you to leave your home. But it is time for you to see wisdom and reason, and to live safely. Leave the farming to someone else. You can still work the land, have a garden. But you cannot continue as now. Even with Matthew's help."

A nurse pushed a mobile cart with a small computer into the room, and the men fell silent.

"Mr. Miller, the cardiologist will stop by soon to talk about the tests he'd like to do." The nurse checked Abraham's vital signs on the machine. She entered them into the computer. "How are you feeling?"

"I'm ready to have a cuppa coffee, and I could do with an early supper." Abraham stroked his beard.

The nurse smiled. "Well, I suspect the coffee will be decaf, but I can see about you getting supper soon. If I were you, I would not expect to go home today."

Abraham frowned. "We'll see about that."

His brother waited until the door closed behind the nurse on her way out before continuing. "If they are keeping you for tests, perhaps it is not as simple a matter as low blood sugar."

Matthew stepped up to support Abraham, even though it was against his father. "I promise you, I have done my best to help Abraham. Today was an unfortunate accident. The district is gathering to help replace the barn roof very soon—as soon as it dries out from the rain." He tried to make his case, but his Daed looked skeptical.

"I don't doubt you have been good for my stubborn brother.

But I want him to understand, once and for all, that something must change."

Abraham waved at them from where he lay on the bed. "I am here. Do not speak about me as if I am not in the room. This morning, I told Matthew that this is my last growing season. I am not putting in a fall crop. What is in the fields now is my last planting."

"Very good. At last, you admit it's time." Daed stopped pacing for a moment. "My wife and I will come for the roof repair. She will help you go through your belongings to see what you will take with you."

"Take with me? Where?"

"To live with us, in Wolfesboro. Matthew can stay at the house until the rest of the fields are finished."

"I'll decide when and where I will move. And I will do so when I am ready."

"You cannot be left by yourself. Even if Matthew is out in the field working, how will he know that something has not happened to you while he is not there?"

"I am not a Kinner."

"Nobody is saying you are a child. If I must bring the bishop in, I will."

"You cannot do that." Abraham's voice was sharp, and the heart monitor's pace increased. "It is my house and I will decide for myself when it is time to go."

The door swung open, again interrupting their conversation. In came a doctor, if Matthew judged correctly. He wasn't wrong.

The man wore a beard himself, but it was trimmed close to his face. He also wore a pleasant smile. "Mr. Miller, I'm Dr. Bridges. How are you feeling?"

"I feel fine, I'm ready to go, and I'm hungry," Abraham grunted.

"We'd like to have you stay with us overnight to run a few tests on your heart." Dr. Bridges pulled a device from his pocket and pushed a few buttons. "Your EKG looked a little concerning—it's a recording of your heart rate—so we'd like to check to make sure there's no blockage. To do that, we need to send you for a special scan and to see what is going on with your blood vessels. If there is a blockage or partial blockage somewhere, we can insert something called a stent to keep the blood flowing to and from your heart."

Abraham folded his arms. "I don't want it. If it's my time, it's my time. Gött knows when that will be."

Matthew observed as the cardiologist tried to convince Abraham to stay. The doctor then turned his attention to Abraham's brother and Matthew. "Is there anything you can do to persuade him?"

Abraham's brother raised his hands. "I cannot."

Matthew shook his head. "Abraham, would it make you feel better to know what is wrong, and why you collapsed? It might be nothing, but then it could be something important. I have a feeling the tests that the doctor is recommending are important. If the tests are fine, then you're fine."

Abraham looked skeptical. "Last time I was told I was dizzy, it was my blood sugar. I felt good this morning. But I did skip breakfast. And nobody told me if they checked my blood sugar when I got here. If I can just have something to eat, I'll feel better. I'm sure of it."

Dr. Bridges frowned. "The only way I can let you leave is if you sign paperwork, agreeing that you are leaving against medical advice."

"Well, then, please bring that paper to me so I can sign it and go home. We have work to do."

Almost an hour later, they were headed home in Daed's buggy. Abraham complained the whole way that "those women" had bypassed going to Louisa Hilty's and instead had brought him to the English doctors, miles and miles and miles away.

"How much will this cost me? I am thankful for everyone's kindness, but this was not necessary. I simply did not have enough to eat this morning. In fact, after I finished the laundry, I was planning to eat a big meal. I was hungry." Abraham finished his speech with a grunt.

He then looked at Matthew. "What do you think? You've been awfully quiet."

"I don't know that it matters what I think, Abraham," Matthew replied. "I want to know that you are all right and you're safe. I'm sorry this happened because of me."

"Because of that roof, you mean." Abraham's shoulders drooped. "I should have asked for help with that sooner. I did not know it was that bad. It could have happened to anyone, the roof tumbling in . . . but are the animals all right?"

"They're fine, as best I recall. My head felt very foggy when I left." Aside from the cut on his forehead and a small goose egg, his head reeled from thinking about the encounter with Sarah in the barn. The way she'd run to him, kneeling down in the mud. She'd grabbed his hand—or had he grabbed hers when she knelt? He couldn't remember.

But he distinctly recalled the strength and gentleness in her touch as she checked his forehead, even as his head swam and he fought to stay awake. In spite of his pain and disorientation from the accident, he clearly remembered wanting to kiss her at that moment. As good as he knew that would have felt, he also knew the wish was very wrong. His position here was precarious at best, more now than ever given what had happened to Abraham this morning.

But he was afraid that now Sarah wasn't just in his head, but also in his heart.

8

The mud from Wednesday's rain was all but gone by Saturday, when Katelynn arrived at the farm stand. She didn't have much produce with her, but she did carry a cardboard box. She set it down on the counter in front of Sarah.

Something made of glass clinked inside the box at the same time Katelynn sighed. "Well, I tried making some jam, but I'm not sure I did it right."

Sarah glanced at the box's contents, half a dozen glass jars filled with a red substance. "What did you make?"

"I made hot-cinnamon jam. I didn't want to waste any fruit on it, in case the jam didn't set up right." She frowned.

"Did you follow the directions correctly on the pectin label?" Sarah held up a jar to the light and inspected it.

"I think so. I mixed and stirred everything, let it boil, then I put the jars in the boiling water. I think the lids all popped too." Katelynn removed the remainder of the jars from the box. "I figured if anybody knew if I made it right, you would."

Sarah tapped the jar's lid, then looked at the top of the lid. The surface did appear as though the vacuum effect had made the lid naturally seal. But when she pushed on the lid's center, it still had a bit of give.

"I'm not sure of this one either. Of course, the jam might not go bad since it's made of red hots and not fruit. Still . . ." She didn't want to say she wouldn't try eating it in a few months. "I'm sure it's good right now. You should probably eat this one first."

Katelynn nodded. "I tasted some of the mixture after it cooled, and it's yummy. But I've been thinking about making jars of jam and other preserves for Christmas gifts, and to sell here at the farm stand. If I made different flavors than you, we wouldn't compete against each other."

"Maybe we can work on jams together sometime. You can help me with apple butter when it's time to harvest," Sarah offered.

"I'd like that. Let's figure out a day and make it happen. I'll buy everything." Katelynn smiled. But her eyes looked worried.

"Are you okay this morning, other than wondering about the jam?" Sarah studied her face.

"It's my brother." Katelynn's shoulders sagged. "Things have gotten worse with him. I don't like to talk about it. It's my family's trouble, and I don't want to worry you with it."

Sarah began to unload her own produce from the handcart outside. "Sometimes, we feel better if we talk about things."

Katelynn seemed to take Sarah's comment as permission to unload. "Well, first, Keith lost his job. He hurt his back, and the construction foreman where he works—or worked—let him go two weeks ago."

"Oh, that's too bad."

Katelynn nodded. "I had never seen him so excited about a job before. But now, in the meantime, he's been doing odd jobs that he can handle physically while he looks for something else."

She fell silent as she stocked the shelves with produce.

"But there's something else wrong too," Sarah said, gently.

"Well, he moved back in with us, and I think he stole from me." Katelynn sighed again. "This morning I left twenty dollars on the corner of my dresser because I wanted to go by the bank and get singles so we can make change today. I went to the kitchen to get a cup of coffee, and when I came back, the money was gone. Of course, no one else had seen it. I looked everywhere, thinking it might have fallen on the floor, behind my dresser, or somehow slid underneath."

"Did you ask Keith about it?"

"Keith insists he didn't see it anywhere when I asked him before I left."

"Well, if he took it, that's not good." Sarah couldn't imagine having a family member steal from her. People helped each other in her community and in her family. But they didn't tolerate stealing, and she couldn't remember the last time anything like that had happened among them—that she knew of anyway. Her thoughts went to the tampered-with cashbox not long ago. Keith had shown up later that same morning. His appearance might not have been a coincidence, especially when viewed in the light of the suspicion Katelynn had just voiced.

"I don't like feeling like I have to watch my things in my own house, well, my parents' house. Mom said we need to be patient with him, that Keith's trying to turn things around. That's what she said before this happened, anyway." Katelynn let out a pent-up breath. Her hand brushed a stack of cucumbers that threatened to tumble from the top of the bin. "Oops."

"I'm sorry you are going through this, especially with a family member. I will pray that God helps him and helps you with the wisdom about what to do."

"Well, thank you. It feels as though it is going to take an act of God for him to change his ways." Katelynn sighed. "Speaking of stealing, on the bright side, it doesn't look as though anyone has tried to break open the box anymore, not since we moved it to the inside of the stand."

"I'm glad. It was easy enough to do. Daed didn't mind at all, especially when I told him why we wanted the change."

A bright-blue pickup truck rolled to a stop at the edge of the driveway. The driver's side window lowered. *Keith.*

He grinned at them both. "Hey, Katie-bug! Can I see ya for a second?"

"I bet his ears must be burning," Katelynn muttered. "Hang on, I'll be right back." She marched over to where the truck sat idling on the side of the road.

Sarah watched the exchange of conversation. With her back to Sarah, Katelynn raised her hands to shoulder level, then nodded. Keith frowned. His face took on a pleading expression. Then Katelynn trotted back to the stand while Keith waited.

"Keith has a job interview in Jackson at eleven today. It's a really good job. But he needs gas money. He has a few dollars but needs more." Katelynn reached for her purse. "If he's got a job interview, that's one thing. A good thing. Because once Keith has money coming in regularly, he'll be out of my hair and maybe on his way to his own place again. I'll give him ten dollars if it helps make that happen."

She pulled a bill from her wallet, then headed back to the truck. Keith accepted the money, a wide grin on his face, and drove off. His truck's horn blared a succession of short honks. Sarah was grateful that no buggies were on the road at that moment.

Katelynn returned, her expression apologetic. "I'm sorry if I sounded uncaring just now. I know the Amish are all about caring for people, especially their own families. I see how the members of your community help take care of each other. But sometimes it's different out in the English world."

"It's all right. I know you love him." She didn't say what she was thinking, which was that Keith had plenty of money for gas now if he'd stolen from his own sister earlier today, in addition to asking her for money now. Katelynn wasn't stupid. She must have thought of that herself but decided to go along with him for her own reasons.

"I do. And that's what makes it hard." Katelynn's smile brightened.

"Anyway, enough about that. I'd like to talk about something happier. What would you think about being a bridesmaid in my wedding?"

Sarah paused where she stood, arranging the last of that day's tomatoes in baskets. "In your wedding?"

"Yes. Do the Amish weddings have bridesmaids?"

"Not exactly, not like English. But I know what a bridesmaid is." Sarah had seen fancy wedding dresses on magazine covers. Some of them were lovely, but some were extremely inappropriate for any woman to wear, Amish or otherwise.

"My mawmaw is sewing my bridesmaids' dresses and has enough fabric to sew three. If I can borrow one of your dress patterns, my mawmaw can sew a cape dress in my wedding colors. So it's a yes, then?"

Sarah hesitated—not because she didn't want to, and not because she didn't think of Katelynn as a friend, but because she had never heard of an Amish person standing up for an English person's wedding.

"I'm not sure. I'm humbled that you've asked me to stand with you. Can I let you know? I'd like to talk to my Mamm about it first."

Katelynn nodded. "Of course. You're a friend, and when I sat down to think about who I wanted in my wedding party, I would like you to be part of it, and be part of one of the most important days of my life."

"Oh, I am honored that you asked me. Thank you, thank you for asking me." Sarah smiled. "I do have a cape dress pattern and a pattern for an apron. I can lend them to your mawmaw, and I can give you my measurements. But I'm not sure that I would be able to stand up with you."

Sarah wanted to explain, but it sounded as though she were a child. Some things weren't a simple yes or no, not like they might be to an outsider.

"That's okay! I know you have your own traditions and rules and stuff, and of course, I don't want to ask you to do anything you shouldn't. But I'm so happy you'll at least consider it." With that, she gave Sarah a sisterly hug.

Sarah found Katelynn's grin infectious and wore one of her own. "I'm very happy for you. You still have a lot to do between now and February."

"Yes, but so far it's been fun, and it's going to keep being fun. I can promise you that." Katelynn resumed lining up her vegetables on the shelves. She slid Sarah a sideways glance. "Now, what's happened to your next-door-neighbor friend? Not the old one, but the one who's new in town? Matthew, I think it is."

Sarah paused. "I haven't seen him in several days, not since earlier this week. I suppose he's doing well. The rain set them back from a few things on the farm, as it did for us. I imagine he's busy."

It was just as well she hadn't seen Matthew since that rainy, soggy day. She'd scrubbed and scrubbed her dress and apron until all traces of the mud had been erased, but she couldn't forget what it had been like to hold his hand. Her curiosity about him had been replaced with something more. And that wasn't good. Not good at all. Because he was only temporary here, and he hadn't been baptized. He could leave anytime.

That evening, while washing the dishes and cleaning the kitchen after supper, Sarah decided to broach the subject of Katelynn's wedding. The dress color itself would be a deep, dark red—in keeping with the English tradition of Valentine's Day.

"Katelynn has invited me to be in her wedding, as one of her bridesmaids," Sarah said as she and Mamm cleared the table.

"*In* her wedding? As part of the procession?" Mamm stopped where she stood as she scraped the leftover salad into a bowl.

"Jah. Her grandmother is sewing her dresses, and she offered to use a pattern and sew a cape dress for me in the same color." As much as she wanted to be there for her friend, Sarah couldn't help feeling she'd be uncomfortable in the role of bridesmaid. She was rather hoping her mother would tell her no.

"Ah, I see." Mamm began putting away the leftovers, which would make a *gut* meal tomorrow on Sabbath. "Well, you are a grown woman. I can't tell you not to go. But I'm not sure of what your father would think, and in the end, you answer to the bishop."

Sarah nodded, though her mother hadn't given her quite the answer she'd hoped for. "Perhaps I'll speak with Bishop at the next singing at the Hiltys' house." That would give her some time to think about it and perhaps she wouldn't need to speak with him at all.

There was to be another singing in the meantime—tonight, in fact. Her thoughts turned to Matthew. Was he recovered enough from his accident to attend? But she knew it was more than an interest in his health that made her long to see him. It was nearly impossible to put him from her mind these days.

The remainder of the week, after his accident in the barn, had passed in a blur for Matthew. He'd had a dull headache that made it difficult for him to attend to his chores, but he was here to help Abraham and help he would.

He couldn't help worrying about his uncle, who stubbornly continued to insist that his heart was fine.

Tomorrow, Sunday, the two had an invitation to Bishop and Mrs. Hilty's home to join them for the noon meal, although there was no worship meeting of the fellowship. Mrs. Hilty would probably send them home with leftovers to see them through a few days the following week, for which Matthew was grateful. Neither Abraham's nor his own cooking skills had improved.

The longer he lived with Abraham, Matthew realized that he just didn't like to cook. Before moving in with Abraham here in Apple Creek, Matthew had stayed with his parents upon reaffirming his faith and requesting to rejoin the district. His Mamm had kept them well-fed.

When Matthew was among the English, living as one of them, he had used the microwave diligently and enjoyed takeout and fast food, particularly Asian food. A microwave was out of the question now, but perhaps he could get takeout or fast food occasionally from town, and bring it back to the house? Surely that wouldn't be forbidden, as long as it wasn't an everyday thing.

Today had been a long day of work, not just taking care of the chores to include the animals, but doing the laundry, a job that Abraham had gladly turned over to his nephew.

Matthew settled onto the front-porch chair opposite Abraham's. Was it his imagination, or did his back just creak as he sat down? Or maybe it was the wooden chair complaining.

"Abraham, I almost feel as if I am the one who's growing old," Matthew observed. He stretched his legs out in front of him on the porch.

"It's the hard work. All those years among the English, and you forgot what it was to put in a true day's effort."

"Ha! I worked plenty. I laid roofs, tile, repaired homes. The Amish don't have a monopoly on hard work." Matthew chuckled, unoffended. An English construction crew had been one of his most labor-intensive jobs.

Abraham gave his own soft chuckle. "Yes, you have worked hard, I'm sure. I was merely poking fun."

Matthew didn't always know when the older man was teasing him, and this was one of those moments.

"You are going to the Hiltys' tonight?" Abraham asked.

Was there a meeting he'd forgotten about? Had the knock on the head knocked out some of his memory? He hadn't thought so . . .

"The singing. Did you forget? Louisa is hosting a singing, tonight, at seven, for the young people." Abraham's eyes twinkled. "Or, as you said, maybe you *are* getting old."

"Ah, the singing." Yes, Matthew *had* forgotten about that. Yes, he was still young although he already had expressed doubts about that a moment ago due to his creaking back. "Maybe I will go."

"Sometimes, I forget you are young. A young man like you should make the time for some enjoyment with other people his age. And maybe you will meet someone or get to know someone better." At that, Abraham's eyes shone brighter. "Then you will have someone to cook for you and you won't end up like me, eating cold food and doing your own laundry in a wash bucket on the porch."

"There is that." Although, with his situation presently, Matthew knew it wasn't the best idea to be entertaining thoughts of courting anyone, let alone someday having someone to cook for him. Matthew stood up and stretched his arms above his head. "Maybe you could come along too."

"Nah, I am old, although I do like the songs very much. Oh, the singings we would have back in the day, going on for hours. I was very good at it. It's not pride to admit something if it's true." Abraham's voice took on an almost wistful tone.

"You're right, it's not." Matthew smiled as he nodded at the man's reminiscing. "I'll milk the cow before I leave, if you'd like."

"No, I can take care of the cow." Abraham paused. "Thank you for helping me. There are some in the family who don't understand, but you do. Maybe it's being around all the English and their odd ways that make you different."

"I think you need to be listened to, Abraham. If you don't want to leave your home just yet, you don't want to. But I know the others are just trying to help. They want to make sure you're safe."

"Help me? Safe?" Abraham snorted. "My brother doesn't come around in months, and this week, I've seen him—what?—three times, not counting the day at the hospital. Now the two-hour trip doesn't seem to bother him. He wants the land. But I don't want him to have it."

Matthew wasn't sure how to take that. This was his own father Abraham was talking about. And if Abraham didn't want Daed to have the land, did that mean he didn't want Matthew to buy it either? Not that he was at all that sure farming was right for him anyway. "How do you know he wants it? Has he come right out and said that?"

"No, but he wants it, just the same. He wants me to move in with him and give him the property so he can sell it or rent it out. But no. I'm not dead. I could have another twenty years left in me, the way we Millers age." Abraham stood, his joints popping as he did so.

"But the farm?"

"Oh, I've decided to sell it. I know my brother won't buy it from me, because he would rather I just deed it to him. No, I've decided to sell it and I have the perfect buyer already in mind."

"Who's that?" The hope faded in Matthew's heart, that Abraham would sell the acreage to him, if he wouldn't sell to his own brother. But somehow, it didn't bother him all that much.

"I think Stoltzfus next door would be happy to add this land to his family's property. I could then have money to purchase a small home in Florida and live there, and the land here would still be owned by an Amish family." Abraham eyed him.

"I can see how that would benefit Mr. Stoltzfus and his family."

Matthew wondered if, perhaps, Levi did purchase Abraham's land, he would allow Matthew to rent just the house from him, at least for a while until he decided where he would settle down.

"Don't look so disappointed, Matthew. Despite my jokes, you are still young. As I've said before, I don't think this is your place to be, not for good." Abraham stepped down from the porch. "Gött will work His will for you."

Matthew watched his uncle head across the yard. Maybe he was right, but if he wasn't here at the farm, what was left for him in Apple Creek?

Sarah.

She was here. He closed his eyes. The longer he stayed, the harder it was going to be to leave her. Perhaps he shouldn't go to the singing.

Except an inner voice told him that maybe the singing was exactly where he needed to be.

9

"Come in, come in!" Mrs. Hilty called out to the young people scaling the steps of her farmhouse. "We have plenty of room and plenty of food."

Sarah took the steps behind Lydia, whose feet seemed to barely touch the wooden surface as she walked beside Thad Graber.

They stepped into the front room, the furniture of which had been shifted to allow for two wooden benches for more seating in addition to the couch and two armchairs. The room quickly filled with at least twelve or thirteen of them, Sarah guessed. Greetings were exchanged and news flew. Tomorrow, Sunday, there would not be a worship service meeting so most families would be staying home unless they had made supper plans elsewhere.

A familiar figure filled the doorway. Matthew Miller scanned the room. He'd removed his hat, and Sarah could see part of the patch on his forehead from the wound inflicted earlier in the week by the falling roof timbers.

"Matthew, you made it," said Louisa. "Please, come in. You've had quite the week. How are you feeling now?"

"Much better, thank you." His glance flicked toward Sarah, whose heart skipped a beat.

"How is Abraham?" Louisa asked.

"He's doing well too, as far as I can tell."

Sarah watched him enter the gathering as some of the others, who appeared to not have heard what happened, exclaimed over his injury and talked about the upcoming roof repairs.

Sarah felt a gentle pressure on her arm. Lydia.

"So you drove yourself tonight?" Lydia asked her.

"What's that?" Sarah turned to face her friend.

"You drove yourself, from your house, by yourself."

"Yes, I did. I brought a lantern for the way home." She settled onto the empty space on the bench beside Lydia. "It'll only be fifteen minutes' ride, if that, and it won't be very dark yet when I leave."

"We would have picked you up, if we'd had the room." Lydia glowed. But Thad had given Lydia a ride to the singing in a courting buggy, with only enough seating for two. It wasn't enclosed, like the larger buggies, allowing the two young people to sit quite close together.

"No matter. I'm just glad we're all here." Sarah's gaze drifted back toward Matthew. He'd ended up sandwiched between two couples on the bench across the room from her. He was talking with James Troyer, who was currently not betrothed to anyone, but everyone knew that Faith Oberholtz, wearing her Sunday-best dress tonight, had her Kapp set for him.

The scenario made Sarah smile, the way couples formed around here. When a young man you hadn't spoken to since your schooling days approached you after your eighteenth birthday, you automatically knew why. He saw you as a potential wife and wanted to see how things went. And the same went for a young woman, who might linger conveniently nearby after a Sunday service. Or, as in the case tonight, at a singing.

"All right," Mrs. Hilty announced. "I have coffee prepared in the kitchen, along with lemonade, some cookies and a few sandwiches for those of you who still have an appetite after supper. Please, help yourselves at any time."

The Hiltys' daughter Mary was in attendance with her husband, who'd come from Wolfesboro a few years ago to marry the bishop's daughter and stay in the community. No one could miss the fact that Mary was with child, and although the couple was married, and married couples didn't usually go to singings, their presence this evening wasn't so odd. They were simply a couple visiting her parents.

Perhaps, Sarah mused, Mary missed her days before marriage, when she could go to events like singings instead of facing the full responsibilities of married life.

Thad, the best singer out of the lot of them, led off with "Amazing Grace." Someday, when they were all much older, he would likely lead the songs during Sunday meetings after the current leader passed the torch or passed away.

Sarah loved the singing, the sounds of voices raised in varying harmonies that filled the room tonight. When she opened her eyes, they fell on Matthew. He wasn't singing. Perhaps he couldn't remember the words. His expression was slightly sheepish.

Their eyes met, and it was as if he guessed she knew he didn't quite know the words. A smile played at the edges of his mouth. Sarah was the first to glance away, her face shot with heat. She'd wondered about him this week, if he had fared well since being clobbered with falling boards in the barn.

They began another hymn, one of her favorites.

Everlasting Father in heaven,
I call on you so ardently,
Do not let me turn from you.
Keep me in your truth
Until my final end.
O God, guard my heart and mouth,
Lord watch over me at all times,

Let nothing separate me from you,
Be it affliction, anxiety, or need,
Keep me pure in joy.

Although she knew the words well, Sarah paused to let the lines linger in her mind, "Keep me pure in joy." She clung to the faith that comforted her, even in uncertainties.

The last notes seemed to hang in the air, and they all smiled when they finished the hymn.

"Please, take a break and eat," Mrs. Hilty said from where she stood in the doorway to the kitchen. "It is only the bishop and me, and we cannot eat all this food I have laid out on the kitchen table."

Sarah chuckled as she stood and stretched. They'd been sitting for a bit, singing song after song. One by one, they filed into the kitchen where they surrounded the plates of sandwiches and cookies.

Lydia and Thad kept up their own conversation where they stood by the stove, and Sarah tried not to feel left out. She was happy for her friend, though. Lydia had had an inclination toward Thad for a long time. More than once, she'd wondered aloud to Sarah if anything were to come of it and lamented the fact that she couldn't just saunter up to him and not so subtly make her interest known.

"Because that would be so brazen," Lydia had said.

But it appeared she hadn't had to worry. Lydia and Thad made a good couple, and Sarah was very happy for her friend. She wouldn't be surprised if the pair of them decided to publish an engagement announcement before too long. They would probably wed before the new year, and then the two would most likely move into a home built for them by either her parents or his, or both.

But then, Sarah had another wedding to look forward to—Katelynn's. The idea of just attending an English wedding—let alone walking down an aisle in a bridesmaid's dress—made her feel a bit nervous, even now as she stood among her people. They had plenty of music, dancing, and alcohol at English weddings, she'd heard. She still wasn't sure if she even wanted to bring the matter up to the bishop. In fact, now that she considered the matter, she was pretty sure there was no need to do so.

"Hello."

Sarah was so caught up in her thoughts, she almost dropped her cup of coffee at the sound of Matthew's voice beside her elbow. She smiled at him. "Matthew. You look as if you feel much better than when last I saw you."

"I am much improved from a few days ago." He, too, sipped from a coffee cup. "I'd almost forgotten Louisa's invitation until my uncle reminded me earlier. It's, ah, been a long time since I've been to a singing. I remember some of the songs, but a few of them, not very well."

"I noticed. I mean, I noticed that you were trying to remember the words—not that you don't have a good voice." She helped herself to a cookie.

Matthew smiled at her words. "Actually, if it's not sounding too prideful, I can carry a song rather well."

"I'm sure you can."

She found her feet felt almost as light as Lydia's appeared when they all filed back into the living room. When they separated, she fought off the tiniest bit of disappointment that didn't stay small, but built inside her instead. Ah, well. She ought to have known. It wasn't a good idea, musing over Matthew as Lydia had over Thad.

A few more songs were sung, and then Sarah spotted a few yawns throughout the room. Then she found her own yawn escaping her, in response. The clock chimed the nine o'clock hour. Not late by an English timetable, she'd heard, but the Amish rose early in the morning.

Lydia was the first to mention leaving. "Well, I suppose it's time to be heading home."

She smiled a wide grin at Thad, who grinned back at her. Sarah wondered how long their journey home would take by buggy.

A few of the others agreed and began saying good night. Lydia gave Sarah a hug.

"I'll see you soon—at quilting this week?"

"Yes, same time." Sarah watched as the two headed for the door. Now it was her turn to say good night to Louisa.

"Thank you for inviting me. It was a very nice evening and so good to be out."

Louisa beamed. "Danke, Sarah. We are always glad to have you here."

Sarah said her other goodbyes, while Matthew continued to speak with Louisa's son-in-law. *Enough*, she told herself. *Stop watching for him like a lovelorn girl.*

She headed out into the moonlit night. Thankfully, the remaining clouds had drifted away so the moon would aid the lantern on Sarah's way home.

"Wait."

Sarah turned around to see Matthew coming down the front steps.

As soon as Matthew called out for Sarah to wait, the rest of his voice stuck in his throat. He made it down the Hiltys' porch steps and joined Sarah on her walk to her buggy.

He glanced toward the driveway, where Thad Graber and Lydia Fry could be seen heading toward the road. A lantern flickered in the late-summer night. A hint of chill drifted with the evening breeze, an early reminder that fall would soon be coming their way.

Matthew shivered as he found his voice. "May I accompany you home?"

Sarah paused at the two-seater buggy. "I . . . I'm not sure." He heard the hesitation in her voice. He hadn't asked her father if such a thing would be allowed—although she was a bit old to ask anyone else but herself for permission. He wanted Levi to approve but knew that likely would not happen.

"I'll even walk beside the buggy, if you would prefer I do that."

"No, you don't have to walk beside the buggy. That's silly." She shook her head.

Matthew patted the horse's neck before continuing. "I can hold on to the back of the buggy and stand on the axle, if that sounds better to you."

At that, Sarah laughed. "Matthew Miller. I never know what you are going to say next." Even in the pale moonlight, he could see the sparkle in her eyes.

"Please, I'd like to see you home. And I have an ulterior motive: I don't want to walk home by myself."

She laughed again. "Are you afraid of the dark?" Her voice was teasing.

"No. Just of what might lie in wait on the side of the road in the dark."

"All right. Let's go." Sarah climbed onto the buggy seat, then picked up the reins. She deftly maneuvered the buggy around so it faced the driveway and the road.

"Start out slowly, then I'll get on the back."

She cast a glance over her shoulder at him, smiling and shaking her head as she did so. The horse moved forward and so did the buggy. Matthew gave a little hop. His boots caught hold on the axle, first one and then the other.

He gripped the back of the two-seater buggy, his hand grazing the top of her shoulder. "Sorry about that."

"It's quite all right. I wouldn't want you tumbling into the road."

They rumbled along the driveway, the cool night air rushing past them. When they reached the edge of the road, Sarah reined the horse to a halt.

"This is silly." She patted the empty seat beside her. "Come, sit here next to me. The ride is but a few minutes, and we don't have any reason to continue this pretense any longer."

No, they didn't.

Matthew stepped down from the rear of the buggy and climbed up onto the seat. He fit snugly into the space, and the angle of the seat made his body lean closer to Sarah's.

What to do with his left arm, now that it was leaning against her while she tried to drive? The easiest, most natural position for his arm would be to lay it across the back of the seat behind her. But that was out of the question, no matter how much he longed to do just that.

"Um, I can see why they sometimes call this a courting buggy," was all he managed to say as he tried to shift away from her. He settled for folding his arms across his chest.

"It isn't a courting buggy. It's just a bit, ah, narrow," Sarah said softly.

She urged the horse forward again, and they were on their way, the horse's hooves making a rhythmic *clip-clop* on the paved road. The lantern swung back and forth on its holder with each gentle sway of the buggy.

"Good night!" a female voice called out behind them.

Sarah raised her right hand and waved, calling out, "Good night, Lydia!"

He could hear Lydia's laughter and the murmur of voices. Sarah would likely hear some teasing about her passenger from Lydia later. She wondered how Thad and Lydia had ended up behind them. Perhaps they'd gone in the opposite direction then circled back to make the ride last longer.

The sound of the hooves was almost like keeping time to a song, and with his nerves on edge, Matthew began to hum his favorite hymn, "*Das Loblied.*" That one, at least, he remembered. But the tempo of the horse's hooves was faster than the traditional song, so he hummed a variation.

"That sounds like a hymn I know, but not like it," Sarah said.

"Yes, it doesn't fit the rhythm of the horse so I changed the tune a little."

"You have a very good hum." She laughed, softly.

"*Danke.*" Maybe it was because of the darkness or because of who was beside him, but Matthew ventured to sing the first verse, regardless of the accompanying hoofbeats.

O Lord Father, we bless thy name,
Thy love and thy goodness praise;
That Thou, O Lord, so graciously
Have been to us always.
Thou hast brought us together, O Lord,
To be admonished through thy word.
Bestow on us thy grace."

Then there was only the music of the horse's hooves and the sounds of crickets. The glow of hundreds of fireflies lit the nearby fields.

"You do have a beautiful voice, Matthew Miller, if you don't mind me saying so. Or should I say, a handsome voice?"

He could scarcely hear the words, though she sat close to him. "Thank you. I hope you didn't mind that I sang. I don't know why I did. Perhaps it was to make up for not singing much at the Hiltys.'"

"I'm glad you sang for me. I like your voice, Matthew."

"Thank you." He wanted to tell her there were many things he liked about her too. That he wished he could sing to her every day. But he didn't say it. He'd been caught up in the songs tonight and all the good memories they brought back to him of being Amish. Yet he wasn't so caught up that he'd forgotten what Abraham had told him today.

If his uncle sold his farm to Sarah's father, where would it leave Matthew?

He listened to Sarah talk about the garden, her progress on the new quilt, and then something else, which caught him off guard.

"My English friend, Katelynn, asked if I would be in her wedding in February. I decided tonight that I would not be an attendant, but I would like to go to the service. I am still a bit nervous, though not as much as I was."

"Nervous? About what?"

"I haven't been around that many English people, all at once. By myself, anyway."

"You will be fine. I am sure of it." He recalled the feeling of being an outsider during his time away. Yes, he'd been surrounded by plenty of English and had grown accustomed to it eventually. But for a young woman like Sarah, he could understand her apprehension now that he thought about it.

"I could still change my mind," she said thoughtfully.

"Well, I hope you do get to go to the wedding ceremony at least. You don't have to stay for the reception if you don't want to." He shook his head. There was no harm in going to an English wedding. None at all.

Sarah went silent and he sensed a shift in her mood. Had he said the wrong thing? If he had, he couldn't think what it was, unless . . . had talking about a wedding—any wedding—made her uncomfortable? He took a deep breath and decided to ask, even though he wasn't sure he wanted to hear the answer.

"Sarah? Is something wrong?"

The horse plodded along a few more yards before she spoke. "It's just . . . I thought I was going to be married, once. But Jacob decided to marry my sister instead." She kept her eyes on the road in front of them.

So that was the cause of the underlying sadness he sometimes sensed in her. He reached over and laid a hand on her arm. She didn't pull back.

What should he say? The simplest thing was all he knew. "I'm so sorry." But it was her sadness he was sorry for, the fact that she had clearly been hurt. He couldn't quite bring himself to be sorry that she wasn't married.

"They seem happy enough. I do my best to be happy for them. It's gotten easier, as time passes, even though I still don't know why his feelings changed," she said, slowing the buggy at an intersection. She wiggled the reins, and the horse turned the corner. "But they did, and here I am. So, what was it like, being among the English for so long, on your own?" she asked, clearly done with the last topic of conversation.

"It was not easy. Much of the time I felt alone. I didn't know their ways at first. But I didn't fit among the Amish either. I questioned where I belonged." He thought of Rebecca, and the flicker of memory pained him because he felt responsible for her leaving her family in Wolfesboro to begin with. He shoved the thought aside and continued.

"Remember I said I had done work for a Mennonite contractor in Ohio? I was there for more than a year. Those were good days, a transition of sorts. Being among the Mennonites made me long for a simpler way of life, and I realized I wanted to come back here to Tennessee to see if I could rejoin our district."

The glow of lantern light from the farmhouse ahead of them lit the darkness with tiny squares. The cornstalks moved in green-gray waves as a few of them caught some of the glow from the moon.

"Almost home," Sarah announced. He couldn't decide if she sounded a little disappointed that their brief journey was coming to the end. He certainly was.

But Matthew wouldn't ask her to lengthen the buggy ride, nor would he discuss possibly going on another one in the future.

If things were different, very different, he could see it happening. Tonight, though, he was just glad she'd agreed to let him ride home with her. This last bit of the trip, he would manage on his own. It was probably better that way anyway. The walk would give him time to think. To try to understand what was happening between him and Sarah—and figure out what to do about it. Because right now, his heart was telling him something that he knew couldn't be. He had to figure out where he belonged before he could bring someone else into his life.

Sarah slowed the buggy as she approached her driveway. "I can continue to your farm. It's not far and I wouldn't be alone for long."

Matthew shook his head. "I'll walk the rest of the way. No need for you to drive in the dark any longer than necessary." Or for them to need to explain anything to either of their families.

She pulled gently on the reins. "Well, then. Thank you, Matthew, for riding home with me. I liked it, very much. I almost hope . . ."

He prayed she wouldn't finish the sentence. The timing was all wrong. Somehow, he thought she knew that too and that's probably why she'd stopped. "You're welcome, Sarah." He got down from the buggy seat. "Have a good night."

Matthew continued along the road toward his own driveway. *What had she been about to say?* He had hopes too, but he didn't see any way to make them come true.

10

The days flew by after the singing until, at last, it was time for the district to visit Abraham Miller's farm to help repair the barn roof. It was mid-September. Soon the leaves would begin to turn colors and the final harvest would be brought in.

This morning was cooler than normal under a bright blue sky. Sarah donned a cardigan. By lunch, it would likely be warm enough to not need a sweater, but for now it was just right.

She pulled the last two pans of her Mamm's sourdough herb bread from the oven. She and her mother had baked ten loaves, and they had plenty of butter in a crock. A large deep pan filled with chicken potpie would go into the oven at the Millers' at the proper time.

"Almost ready?" Mamm asked from where she stood in the kitchen doorway.

"Jah, I just need to wrap the bread after it cools a bit." Sarah fetched some clean towels from the linen drawer, spreading one of them on the table, then tumbled the fresh loaves of bread onto the towel so they could cool.

Within the hour, they had loaded up the food along with Daed's toolbox and other supplies into the buggy, and the three of them headed the short distance to Abraham Miller's farm.

Sarah never mentioned to her parents that on the evening of the singing she'd given Matthew a ride part of the way home from the Hiltys'. She felt a tiny bit of guilt because of that, but then, she was a grown woman, they'd done nothing wrong, and Matthew had been a gentleman. In fact, he'd tried to maneuver himself so the snug fit of the buggy didn't keep him any physically closer to her than necessary. She chided herself when she felt a pang of disappointment.

She smiled to herself at the recollection of him sitting with his knees jutting out the side of the buggy with his arms crossed over his chest.

"Why the smile this morning?" Mamm asked. "Is there someone you're hoping to see today?"

"Not exactly." She knew she'd see Matthew there, so there was no need to hope for that.

"I hear the Hiltys' nephew Jeremiah may be visiting from Wolfesboro, if I remember Louisa telling me correctly. I believe he might be about your age," Mamm said.

"Oh, that's nice. The Millers will have plenty of help for repairing the barn roof with an extra pair of hands."

Mamm laughed. "Maybe Louisa will introduce the two of you to each other. As best I know, he is not married, nor is he engaged or courting anyone."

"Now, Bea," Daed said. "No need to play matchmaker."

"I'm not doing anything of the sort. However, I really do not think Matthew Miller is a suitable man for our daughter."

"Mamm!" Sarah blurted. "There is nothing going on between Matthew and me."

"It's a sin to lie, Sarah," Mamm replied. "I have heard it from more than one person that you left the Hiltys' singing with Matthew Miller, and they wondered about the two of you."

Sarah sucked in a breath as they rounded the turn into the Millers' driveway. Already, at least four buggies were lined up by the pasture fence. Someone had already set up a table beneath a nearby tree and lumber was stacked by the barn.

"Bea, let her be. She is an adult."

"Well, I want her to be careful. Matthew may look as plain as the day is long, but that doesn't mean he *is* plain, in his heart."

"Ah, didn't I tell you, time will tell?" Daed gave Mamm a look, "We will see. 'By their fruit, ye shall know them.' And it is almost harvesttime."

What was her Daed saying? He was not rejecting Matthew outright, which surprised her.

Mamm turned to face Sarah. "I know you are grown, and you can decide for yourself whom you will wed. But watch for men like him. A mother never stops caring for her children, nor does she stop wanting to help them."

"Some things a child needs to do and learn on their own," Daed observed as he pulled the wagon to the nearest clear spot by the pasture fence. "But yet again, a wise one heeds the advice of his parents."

"Thank you, Daed," was all Sarah could manage to say. Evidently no one had hinted at suspicion of any impropriety between the two of them for traveling home together, or she would have gotten an earful. But then, Matthew hadn't finished proving himself to either the Apple Creek or Wolfesboro districts. If the two of them going home together after the singing had been a true concern at this time, Sarah suspected Bishop would have already paid a call on both her and her parents, and on Matthew, at their respective homes. But that hadn't happened.

They all climbed from the buggy. Out in the fresh air, Sarah could breathe more easily.

Or was it because the uncomfortable conversation was over, for now at least? She had a nagging suspicion that the matter was far from finished.

Lydia waved when she caught sight of Sarah, who carried a bundle of bread and the crock of butter. Mamm carried the rest of the loaves of bread, balanced atop the chicken potpie.

"Here we are." Lydia reached for the crock of butter. "The women have already taken over the kitchen inside and are cleaning it just so we can all mess it up again with our lunch preparations."

Sarah nodded, following Lydia up the porch steps, into the front room, and then into the kitchen. It indeed was a hub of activity, with women scrubbing and scouring and sweeping.

"There you are with the bread," said Mrs. Hilty. "Please, put all the food on the large table in the kitchen. We'll have this cleaned straightaway. But you two can help by making the lemonade. We'll need several gallons. You do know how to make it?"

"Yes. I happen to make excellent lemonade, or so I am told." There Sarah was, being prideful again. And in front of the bishop's wife, no less. She cleared her throat. "We're glad to help."

The older woman didn't mention the sin and motioned toward the front of the house. "You'll find several bags of lemons, a sack of sugar, and a container on the porch. If you are efficient, you can have the lemonade finished by the time the men are ready for their first work break."

Sarah and Lydia found the ingredients on the porch and set up work on a long table beneath the trees. Someone had covered the table, made of sheets of plywood perched on sawhorses, with a white cloth.

"Is Thad here?" Sarah asked Lydia as the two began cutting lemons and taking turns using the lemon press.

"Jah, he's over there. So is Matthew." Lydia's tone was teasing, yet gentle.

"Ah, of course Matthew would be here. He lives here, silly." Sarah scanned the small swarm of men positioned on the barn's roof, beside the barn, and some going in and coming out.

There was Matthew, atop the barn. He was using a handsaw, and it appeared he was cutting out old, rotten boards left over from the ones that had fallen in on him.

Matthew motioned and gave directions from where he knelt, although Sarah couldn't make out his voice from where she stood. She returned her attention to slicing the lemons in front of her. No good would come of gaping across the yard—not for her fingers and not for keeping her attention where it needed to be.

She understood her parents' concerns and part of her shared them. If Matthew had been a member of this community, or even of Wolfesboro, for longer, no one would be wondering about him so much. Lydia headed off to the outdoor pump to get some cool water.

An engine's roar filled the air as a car came up the driveway toward the farm. Who else did the Millers expect? It would be quite unusual for English to join in an activity of this sort.

Sarah squinted at the sedan. She glimpsed two figures in the back seat, one wearing a Kapp and the other wearing a straw hat. An Amish couple, then, who must have hired a driver.

The car ground to a halt and the figure wearing the Kapp shot from the back seat.

"Sarah!"

"Emma?" Sarah choked out her sister's name.

Her sister, Kapp strings flying past her shoulders, made a beeline for Sarah, coming at a fast, awkward trot. Her rounded belly probably made it impossible to run, which she clearly wanted to do. When Emma reached Sarah, she enveloped her in a hug.

"Oh, I've missed you so. We're back, back for good. I need you and Mamm right now," Emma whispered into her ear.

Sarah did not let herself glance toward Jacob standing behind her shoulder. Instead, she pulled back and smiled at her sister. The gray cape dress Emma wore hid any evidence of the new life growing inside her, but Emma's cheeks were rounder, fuller, and her face had a subtle glow.

"I've missed you too, Emma."

"I'm so happy we're back. I convinced Jacob not to tell Daed and Mamm we were coming today. You all knew we were coming eventually, of course. But we wanted it to be a surprise." Emma scanned the crowd gathered for the roofing project. "Where are they?"

"Mamm is in the kitchen, and Daed is up there." Sarah looked up to the roof, where two figures worked. Matthew was climbing the ladder with an armload of supplies.

Emma followed her gaze, then gave Sarah a sideways glance filled with mild curiosity. "I don't recognize that man. The very handsome one you can't take your eyes off."

Measure twice, cut once, Matthew repeated the old adage to himself when he returned to his rooftop perch. They had already cut out most of the damaged sections, which turned out to be more than half of the shingles, decking, and even some portions of the support beams. He didn't mind this work, enjoyed it even. The feel of the wood beneath his fingertips, the satisfaction of hammering a nail into a board with just enough force, and the sense of accomplishment that rolled through him as each new area was repaired—this was an area of his life that he could control and take pleasure in.

"We need twelve-by-sixes," said Levi from where he also knelt on the roof. "Looks like these are rotting or rotten. It's a shame. I had hoped we could salvage more of the wood that's already here."

"Jah." Matthew nodded. "I did too. But once we're finished, this roof will last for years to come and no one will worry about leaking or about the roof falling on anyone's head." It didn't look like it would be him, though.

He paused a moment to wipe his forehead with a handkerchief, taking the opportunity to look out over the fields that would lie fallow next year. He still didn't know when he'd be leaving, or where he'd go once the sale went forward. Sad as he would be to see the land leave the Miller family, he couldn't help thinking that maybe Abraham had been right when he told him that farming wasn't the right occupation for him.

Matthew measured the next section of roof where the decking needed replacement. He carefully maneuvered around the yawning space that made a rectangle of light on the dirt floor far beneath them. He tried not to guess how many feet it was from roof to floor, but it didn't matter. Anyone falling from this height would sustain a serious injury.

Right after his accident, he'd moved the cow to a smaller barn on the property, not trusting that more boards wouldn't fall and injure the animal. It would be nice to get her back into her customary surroundings before it began to get really cold. He completed the remainder of his measurements, then tucked the measuring tape, pencil, and his notes into his pocket. The crew on the ground would measure and cut the pieces of wood.

Carefully, Matthew descended the ladder and felt immediately better when he was on solid ground again.

He glanced toward the area where the women were organizing the food and young children played. A small cluster of women teemed together, some of them talking excitedly.

Likewise, a few of the men were gathered in their own cluster, less enthusiastic but still notable enough for Matthew to wonder what the to-do was. They hadn't served lunch yet, nor was it time for a break. Not officially, anyway.

Levi descended the ladder and stood beside him. He squinted, then strode in the direction of the group of men. "Well, if that doesn't beat all. Look who's here."

Matthew trailed along behind him.

"It's Jacob Plank, my son-in-law." He stopped in front of a younger man who had a rather short beard and a head full of hair that looked as if it were trying to escape from under his straw hat.

"Levi." The men shook hands, with Levi clapping Jacob on the arm. "It's good to see you. It's good to see you all. We're back, for good," Jacob said.

"I know, I know. But we didn't expect you today. How is my daughter? Where is she?"

Matthew had never heard Levi's voice so full of animation, not in the space of time he'd known the man.

Jacob laughed, a boisterous sound. "Right over there with the other women. She didn't want to rest at the house, so I had the driver drop off our things and then bring us over here. I saw all the buggies across the way and figured there was some kind of gathering here."

The conversation flowed as the men evidently decided now was a good time to take a break. Matthew fought off the irritation that threatened to well up. No, it wasn't that their work had been delayed. One of the men had taken his large wagon to get more supplies, so they couldn't do much until he returned from the lumberyard anyway.

It was the fact that this man, this Jacob Plank, had hurt Sarah. For some reason, in Matthew's estimation over the brief seconds he'd seen Jacob Plank, he believed the man never deserved her. Perhaps he should be thanking God that Sarah didn't end up with a man like Jacob.

Matthew's conscience chided him as he went to get himself another glass of lemonade. He was passing judgment on a person he did not know, when he didn't like others doing the same thing to him. He didn't know Jacob Plank, other than what Sarah had said. Maybe Jacob should have had the fortitude to tell Sarah why his interest had changed from her to Emma. But he certainly wouldn't be the first man to lose his nerve about having a difficult conversation with a woman.

Matthew found a clean glass and filled it to the top with lemonade. He took a generous gulp. The combination of sweet and sour helped take the edge off his hunger.

Levi was leading Jacob toward the barn, pointing up at the roof as he did so.

"Stoltzfus and I have come to an agreement," Abraham said at Matthew's elbow. "We're going to get a sales contract prepared soon, very, very soon, once we settle on a price. If all goes well, I'll be on my way to Florida before the first snow flies."

The glee in Abraham's voice was obvious.

"You'll enjoy yourself, I'm sure," Matthew said. Now the men headed into the barn. Levi seemed much more excited about the structure than Jacob.

"You could always come to Florida too. There's plenty of work in Pinecraft, I'm sure. I guess I wouldn't mind having you around."

Matthew grinned. He'd grown fond of his uncle too. "Yes, there is. I had good work there, before." And it was a very pleasant place, Pinecraft, at least in the winter months when it wasn't so hot.

"Uh-huh. So what's holding you back now?"

"That's a very good question, Abraham. Not sure if I have the answer for you, just yet." Matthew stared across the yard at the women, who stood in a gathering as they chatted with a young woman in a gray, shapeless dress. He didn't recognize her. He guessed it was none other than Mrs. Jacob Plank, Sarah's sister.

With her stomach full after lunch and her heart full of joy at seeing her sister, Sarah strolled arm in arm with Emma after helping the others see to the cleanup after the meal. The men were already back at work on the barn, among them Jacob and Jeremiah, the Hiltys' nephew.

"So," Emma said, giving her a sideways glance, "about this Matthew…"

"He's our neighbor," said Sarah, wishing her sister would drop whatever it was she was trying to bring up in conversation.

At that, Emma laughed. "Ha! I know that. But what about him? He is unmarried, obviously. And I've noticed how he looked at you during lunch."

Sarah struggled to find the words. Yes, she had feelings for him. But she hadn't let him know in any way that she knew of, that she had more than a mild interest in him. Nor would she. She had a feeling her heart would get broken again if she did so.

"He's a kind man, devoted to Abraham. I . . . like him."

Thankfully, they had strolled away from the others. Sarah hoped no one would begrudge her a few minutes with her sister. She didn't want them to think she was shirking her duties, but she hadn't seen Emma since last Christmas.

"Well, I think he likes you right back, sister." Emma stood still, glancing toward the barn. "And here I was, trying to introduce you to Jeremiah Hilty. Jacob and I know him from Wolfesboro, and I think you'd like him too."

Sarah tried not to fidget. Jeremiah was looking over in their direction. Her interest in him was mere curiosity, as in how long he planned to stay in Apple Creek and why he was here in the first place.

Jeremiah, the bishop's nephew, was not tall nor short, stocky nor thin, and his hair was not brown nor blond. There was nothing that stood out about him, other than bright-blue eyes. "Hilty eyes," someone had called them. Bishop had the Hilty eyes, but his piercing gaze didn't have the gentle warmth that Jeremiah's had.

"He's smiling because you're staring, Sarah."

Sarah sighed and rolled her eyes. "Let's find Lydia. She'll want to see you too."

11

"I could hardly believe what I was seeing. There they were, showing up at the roofing." Sarah peeled an apple. She stood in a cheerful English kitchen, complete with a refrigerator, gas stove, and a dishwasher. The room smelled like fruit and cinnamon, a mouthwatering combination. Today was the promised canning time with Katelynn.

"Wow, just wow." Katelynn shook her head from where she sat at the breakfast bar. She, too, peeled apples. The two had pooled together their produce, some of which had come from the few apple trees at Sarah's farm, the rest from a local orchard Katelynn had visited with her fiancé.

"Jah. I've missed Emma, very much. She and Jacob are now moved in to the empty bedroom in the house. Jacob is busy working with Daed, and Emma helps Mamm around the house too."

"When is she due?"

"Before Christmas. I'm not sure what their plans are, exactly, for moving into their own home. But I'm looking forward to having a new niece or nephew around. Babies are beautiful." Sarah continued to slice the apples, the chunks of which would go into a pot on the stove along with some sugar and a squeeze of a fresh lemon.

"Well, babies might be beautiful, but they're noisy and a lot of work too."

"I want a bunch of them someday—one at a time, of course, God willing." Sarah smiled at her words. Fewer things felt as good in your arms as a new baby. And as the little ones grew, each age held a marvel.

"Well, I'm sure someday you will."

She didn't talk about Matthew, or meeting Jeremiah Hilty, who was as nice as he seemed and did not hide his curiosity about her. When he asked if she'd be at the next singing, she truthfully enough told him she expected to be busy with putting up this year's produce for the winter.

The front door banged open and in came Katelynn's brother, Keith. "Yum, yum, smells like pie in here, y'all." He stomped over to the stove, sniffing as he did so. "Oh, so you're making jelly."

Sarah wondered if Keith had been hired for the job he'd interviewed for. Katelynn hadn't mentioned it, so maybe not. He wore a soiled T-shirt and work pants that had seen better days.

"We're making apple butter," Katelynn said.

"Sign me up for some of that." Keith went to the refrigerator, opened the door and stared inside. "There's no leftover lasagna?"

"No," Katelynn replied. When Keith's back was to her, she looked at Sarah and rolled her eyes. "Mom took the rest of it for her lunch today."

He closed the refrigerator and headed for the bread box. "Can I try some of the jam? It smells really good."

"You can open one of the jars on the table," Sarah said. "It'll be warm, but still good."

"Thanks." Keith helped himself to a dollop of the freshly made apple butter. He pulled out a chair from the table and sat down hard.

The young women turned back around to the stove, with Sarah doing her best to forget about Keith while she watched Katelynn stir the mixture on the stovetop until it boiled. Then, while it was still bubbling, Katelynn filled the next dozen jars. She wiped the rims, placed the lids atop the jars, screwed on the bands, then put the jars one by one into a stockpot filled with boiling water.

"Here," Sarah said. "This is the most important part of all—when the vacuum happens and preserves the fruit. If the lid doesn't pop shortly after it comes out of the water, then the jar's not sealed and that's when your jars can go bad."

"Can I do this for meat too, say when Steven goes hunting?"

Sarah shook her head. "Meat is a different process, and you need a pressure canner to keep the meat from spoiling."

"Whoooo-eeee!" Keith shouted, making both of them jump and turn in his direction. "This is some fine stuff. Tastes like spicy apple pie. You'll be able to sell lots of it, I bet."

"We hope so," Katelynn said. "That, and guess what you'll be getting for Christmas?"

Keith laughed. "I'll take a dozen jars under the tree and four in my stocking. Seriously, did you think about making some real apple pies too?"

"No, we're going to make fake apple pies," Katelynn said with sisterly sarcasm. She turned to Sarah. "When do I take the jars out?"

Sarah looked at the clock on the stove. "Right about now. Use the tongs, then let each jar sit on the counter on a towel."

She let Katelynn remove each of the jars with the tongs. It could be tricky not to burn yourself, if you weren't used to it. "Good. Now watch and listen."

Sure enough, within a few minutes the lid on each of the jars made a popping sound, sealing the sweetness inside. Sarah watched the look of joy on Katelynn's face. She remembered how exciting it had been when she'd made her own first successful batch of apple butter.

"We did it!" Katelynn grinned. "And it wasn't as hard as I thought it would be to get it right. I feel so much better about trying this again. Thank you, Sarah. Really. It's probably not that big of a deal to you, but this is one of the neatest things I've learned to do in a while."

"We'll check the seals by pressing on the lids once they cool a bit.

Didn't your mother ever teach you about cooking and preserving?" Sarah asked.

"Ha!" Keith chortled from across the table. "She taught us about how to call for takeout."

"Keith." Now Katelynn rolled her eyes within both of their view. "She knows how to make spaghetti, fried chicken, lasagna, things like that."

"Nothing like this, though." Keith waved a slice of bread spread with butter and apple butter. "But about the pies. Are y'all going to make some pies for Thanksgiving? It's not too far away from now. Talk about making some money. People would line up to buy them."

Sarah considered that. If she made enough piecrust and Katelynn helped prepare the fruit and pumpkin fillings, they could make quite a few pies and sell them for a nice profit. She didn't know of anyone else in their community who was selling them, so they wouldn't be cutting into another person's business.

"You know, that's not such a bad idea. Katelynn, what do you think? I know I could use the money and I know you can, for sure, since you're paying for a wedding. We can start taking orders now. If customers prepay when they order, we won't be out the money in case anyone changes their minds."

Katelynn carried the empty pan she'd used to cook up the apple butter mixture to the sink. "I know we kinda talked about it once, but if you think we can do it, I'm game."

"We can set a limit of how many pies we will bake and make a menu. I'll get an ingredient list together. And I can add a sign about pies to the one on the driveway advertising the farm stand." Sarah felt a twinge of excitement inside.

If she could save up enough money, she would take that trip to Pinecraft after all. The women would indeed have two quilts for the auction, and Sarah could transport them herself.

The excitement between Katelynn and Sarah buoyed her spirits all the way home in Katelynn's truck. She waved goodbye, then went inside the house to find Emma.

Her sister was crocheting what might have been the beginning of a baby blanket as she sat near a small, simple side table holding a spare ball of yarn in a soft yellow. Emma's feet rested on a stool. Her feet and ankles had begun to swell, and she was following the midwife's instructions to elevate them as much as she could.

Emma looked up from her work. "Did you have fun with your English friend?"

"I did. Today, she learned how to make apple butter."

"I think it is funny how the English think they can be like us by making their own jelly and things like that."

Sarah wasn't sure how to take the comment from her sister, so she ignored it. For a few seconds. "Katelynn isn't trying to be Amish. She simply wanted to learn how to make a few things. So, I taught her. It was easy enough." Sarah took the other empty chair in the room.

"I'm sorry." Emma frowned. "I haven't been sleeping well, and Jacob has been all in a mood since we arrived here. I'm not sure what is bothering him."

Sarah glanced toward the kitchen. "Where are Mamm and Daed?"

"Mamm is visiting Louisa Hilty, and Daed is over at the Miller farm with Jacob. It's just us here right now."

Sarah struggled to find the words to talk to her sister. It was as though Emma had truly come home, but she wasn't the same Emma as before she married and moved to Wolfesboro. Although, from time to time Sarah did see glimmers of the joyful sister she had known.

"Oh!" Emma placed her hand on her stomach. "The baby moved. Come, feel her kick."

"Her?" Sarah crossed the room and knelt by her sister's chair.

"I'm just saying that. Jacob says it's a boy. We'll see." Emma smiled as she reached for Sarah's hand. "Right here. I think that's her feet."

Sarah felt the movement beneath her hand. "How wonderful. It's truly a miracle."

"No, not a miracle. It's the way God makes people grow, my dreamer of a sister." Emma picked up her crochet hook again and wove the yarn through her fingers.

Sarah moved back to her chair and sat down, deciding to change the subject. "My farm stand is doing well. Katelynn and I decided today that we're going to start taking pie orders for Thanksgiving. I'm very excited about it. Even after the stand is closed when harvest is done, we'll still be making money."

Emma promptly burst into tears. "Ach, Sarah, I'm so unhappy."

If a fellow waited long enough, sometimes a man or two would start talking and telling stories.

Matthew found himself sitting Saturday afternoon on the front porch of the Apple Creek General Store while he watched Herbert Byler and Homer Chupp play checkers.

The day of the roof repairs and reconstruction, coupled with the sudden arrival of Jacob and Emma Plank in Apple Creek, had increased Abraham's eagerness to sell the farm. Matthew's season at the farm was ending, just like the crops that would soon be harvested.

Levi Stoltzfus and Jacob Plank had both paid a visit to the Miller farm earlier that morning, with Levi intending to school Jacob on all things concerning autumn on a farm. The man already knew how to care for the livestock, but there were many things to be done before the winter weather descended. They would probably be talking more about the terms of the sale as well.

"You ready to play a round, young Matthew?" Herbert asked.

"No. I'm more than happy to sit here and visit while the two of you play."

"Will be an interesting sight to see, if young Jacob Plank can run a farm," observed Homer. "I knew the family back in Wolfesboro. Good people, but out of all the Plank boys, Jacob would be the one to lollygag at the end of the line."

Herbert moved his checker and captured one of Homer's. "Now, now, Homer. We all know that people can change over time. Even little boys grow up, as we did."

"Now look at us, with ears almost as long as our beards." The man chuckled, and at that remark, Matthew had to crack a smile.

"You're right, maybe he has changed. I hope for his wife's sake that he has." Matthew took another sip of his coffee. He ought to be getting back to the farm, but he was in no hurry at the moment.

"Now, *that's* a story for you." Herbert settled back on his chair. "Your young friend, Sarah Stoltzfus, she had her eyes on Jacob. Everybody knew that, even though she tried to hide it, and Jacob did too. Then he switched his interest faster than an English man turning on an electric lamp. Poof! It was all Emma after that."

"Herbert, that's old news, and what was done has been done, and no changing it." Homer skipped two of Herbert's checkers with extra vigor. "No sense repeating it, either."

"Well, it bothered me to see Sarah on the short end of things. Everything changed when Jacob went out walking late at night with Emma, and because of that, the girl's parents made him marry Emma instead, to avoid any hint of scandal."

Matthew hadn't heard that part of the story, if it was even true.

"No disrespect, but Sarah told me she never knew why Jacob's, ah, focus changed from her to Emma. Why wouldn't they tell Sarah about something like that?"

Herbert shrugged. "I don't know. Maybe the few who knew wanted to save her the embarrassment. But I do know most of us were surprised when the engagement announcement was published by Jacob and Emma, not Jacob and Sarah."

"Interesting, but Homer has a good point. Nothing can change what happened." Matthew polished off the rest of his coffee, then tossed the cup into the trash container by the front door.

"Yes. Now, looking to the future, I see that a Hilty and Stoltzfus match may be brewing, though," Homer observed. "Jeremiah is a future bishop in the making, I have a feeling, and the Hiltys would like nothing more than to see one of their own, even if a nephew, not a son, become bishop one day."

Matthew felt his chest tighten. Homer could only be talking about Sarah. If something was happening between Sarah and Jeremiah, Matthew needed to know. "What makes you think there will be a match?"

"Everything," said Herbert. He skipped another of Homer's checkers and ended up on Homer's side of the board. "King me."

Matthew nodded. He wasn't going to get any more information from these two. "I'd better be going. Abraham may need me."

Matthew headed for the buggy and then straight for the farm. He arrived home minutes later. Home? For now. Abraham and the Stoltzfuses were out in the pasture, walking toward a cow grazing on the last of the late-summer grass.

Matthew drove to the barn. Brown, true to her docile self, stopped and stood patiently while Matthew unhitched her. By the time he finished stabling the horse and putting the tack away, the other men had assembled on the porch.

"So," he could hear Abraham saying, "have you decided yet?"

Levi Stoltzfus nodded. "I have. Or, I should say, we have. We'll take the evening and discuss it at home, and I'll be back in the morning to bring you an offer."

"Very good, very good." Abraham shook hands with Levi. "This will be just the thing for you. And for me too."

Jacob said nothing but seemed to be staring across the field toward the neighboring farmhouse. He glanced at Matthew briefly, then at the field again.

The two men left, walking briskly down the driveway. Levi clapped Jacob on the back, his voice raised with excitement yet still muffled enough that Matthew couldn't make out the words. Levi seemed much more enthusiastic about the prospect of the farm than Jacob.

"That's that." Abraham nodded. "It's providential, it is. One of the first things I will do in Florida is pick an orange, or maybe a lemon, from a tree. Then I will go to the beach and walk barefoot in the sand."

"I'm glad for you," Matthew said, truthfully enough.

A shiny red car pulled up at the edge of the gate and parked. Matthew wondered if it was a tourist or a local Englisher who mistakenly believed the Millers had something for sale at the farm. Prepared to inform the driver they had nothing to sell, Matthew stepped off the porch and headed for the car.

The driver's door opened and a young woman emerged.

"Matthew—it *is* you!"

He stopped. Stared. "Rebecca?" She bore a physical resemblance to his old friend, one-time girlfriend. But this wasn't the woman he'd known years ago.

Another slam from one of the car doors, and a small boy rounded the back of the car and joined her on the driver's side.

"Mommy, we're here?" The boy looked up at him.

The young woman smiled at her son, and then at Matthew. Her auburn hair fell past her shoulders in bouncing waves. Her complexion held the peaches-and-cream glow he remembered from long ago, not the sallow texture with hollowed eyes from the last time he'd seen her. She looked casual, yet well put together in stylish jeans, black slip-on shoes, and a simple white T-shirt topped with a dark green cardigan. Silver bracelets clinked on one of her wrists.

Matthew found his voice and all he could do was repeat her name. "Rebecca?"

She nodded. "I just missed you at the General Store, I heard. GPS wasn't too helpful in getting me here, and even though your parents wrote out directions for me, I still got turned around for a few minutes."

"You look much . . . happier than the last time I saw you."

"Thanks." She smiled at him. "You look . . . Amish again."

He chuckled, but the sound caught in his throat. "I *am* Amish again."

From behind him, Abraham said, "Well, you going to stand there talking, or are you going to invite your friend inside for some lunch?"

Matthew remembered his manners. "Please, come inside. We don't have a lot, but we can put together at least a sandwich and some fruit, and get you both something to drink."

"Yes, I'd like that." She smiled down at her son. "Right, Dylan?"

"Uh-huh." The boy's focus traveled to the barn. "Can we see the animals after we eat?"

"Of course," Matthew said. He motioned for them to follow him up the stairs and inside the house.

Rebecca Mast, here, in Apple Creek, at the Miller farm. And with a child, no less. Never had he expected such a thing to happen. Not in this lifetime.

12

Abraham puttered around the kitchen, where he made grilled cheese sandwiches and fried potatoes. He apologized for not having ketchup, to Matthew's amusement.

"I know you English Kinner like ketchup, don't you?" Abraham stood at the stove. He had already shooed Matthew to sit at the table with Rebecca and her son.

Matthew couldn't stop staring at Rebecca. She'd been transformed.

"I feel great." Rebecca smiled at him, then at young Dylan. "It's because of this guy here. And because of you."

"Me?"

They paused as Abraham set a plate full of sandwiches between them, followed by a plate of home fries. He waved before moving as if to leave the kitchen.

"Where are you going, Abraham?" Matthew asked. "Please join us."

"I'm going to sit on the porch." He left.

"I remember him, I think. He's the odd uncle in the Miller family, right?" Rebecca smiled as she made a plate for Dylan. "Here you go. You heard Mr. Miller, they don't have ketchup."

"That's okay." The little boy attacked his sandwich.

Rebecca turned her focus back to Matthew. "Yes, it was Dylan and you. I know the last time we saw each other . . . wow, it was really bad. I wasn't sure if I was going to make it. But it wasn't you that got me there. It was me. Nobody made me start drinking except for me."

Matthew shook his head. "I know, but if I hadn't asked you to come with me, to leave Wolfesboro, you wouldn't have strayed as far as you did. You could have died because of me."

"Correction. You're wrong." She took a bite from her sandwich. "Wow, this is good. Nothing beats Amish cheese. No, like I said, you're wrong. I wanted to leave, and when you offered me the chance, I took it. You were my way out of there. If it wasn't you, it would have been someone else I hitched a ride with. You happened to be the first one."

Matthew couldn't eat a bite of the sandwich in front of him. He'd wondered about Rebecca after he left her at a nightclub in Florida a year or so after they'd left Wolfesboro. They'd had a big fight about her drinking. She was fine, she'd insisted. He knew she wasn't, but if she wouldn't accept help, he couldn't force her. Walking away was one of the hardest things he'd ever done.

Almost as if she'd read his thoughts, she said, "You walking away from me was the best thing that ever happened to me. No, second best. Becoming a foster mother to Dylan, then adopting him? That was the best thing." She smiled at her son affectionately. "He just turned five, a few weeks ago."

"Well, you are both blessed to have each other." Matthew looked at the boy. He was adorable, with curly brown hair and big brown eyes.

Rebecca must have seen the questions in Matthew's eyes, because she continued. "Long story short, I got my GED, went to college, and now I'm a social worker for a nonprofit agency. I'm also studying for my professional counseling license. I have a job in Spring Hill, not far from Nashville and a short enough drive from Wolfesboro." Rebecca sighed.

"Have you been back yet? Well, of course you have, if you found me here." Matthew was still trying to grasp the fact that Rebecca was sitting across the kitchen table from him.

Rebecca nodded. "I knew it was time to visit my parents and ask for their forgiveness, which they gave me without reservation and was probably more than I deserve. They fell in love with Dylan, as if he were their own blood grandchild. I want him to get to know them. My parents also suggested I visit you. They were the ones who told me you had come back."

Dylan polished off the last of his lunch. "Can we go see the animals?"

"You bet." Matthew stood, and Rebecca began to clear their plates.

The three of them headed outside, and Matthew led them to the pasture, where the cow grazed. The calf stood not far away. It was not the time of day to try to milk a cow, so Matthew figured the five-year-old might enjoy petting the large animal.

Dylan's eyes were wide and round in his head as Matthew lifted him up so he could pet the cow's head. "He's *big*."

Matthew smiled. "Actually, this one is a female. She gives us milk."

Rebecca laughed. "We haven't had that discussion yet. He thinks all cattle, or cows, are boys."

"Ah, I see. Well, this one is a lady cow, and the other one is her baby. The little one is a boy."

They then headed for the chicken house. To Dylan's delight, he found two eggs, which Matthew said he could carry to the house.

Rebecca also helped collect some of the eggs as they walked back through the farmyard. "I miss this, sometimes. Maybe, one day, when I can buy a house, it'll have a little bit of acreage."

"Can we get a cow too?" Dylan asked.

"I don't know about that." Rebecca laughed. "This has been so nice, Matthew. Thank you for lunch, for listening. It was . . . a little harder to visit Wolfesboro."

Matthew paused at the short picket fence. "I imagine it was. But I'm glad you were able to speak with your parents."

She nodded. "Maybe that's why it was a harder conversation. We've made plans for Thanksgiving. My parents are excited about it. Dylan was like a healing balm between us, but things are a bit awkward still. I have a place at their table since I was never formally shunned, and for that I'm grateful. But I made it clear to my parents I am not joining the church. I'm English now, and I don't plan to give up everything I've worked for."

"I'm glad for all of you." Matthew's throat caught. He'd once loved Rebecca, or thought he had. The strong, accomplished woman in front of him held faint glimmers of the one he'd known long ago.

Rebecca surprised him with a hug and a swift kiss on the cheek. "There, that's for old time's sake. Maybe I'll see you again sometime, if you ever get to Wolfesboro to visit your parents, that is."

"Maybe. Not sure when that'll be. But I'm happy that you stopped by, and that you're doing so well." His throat swelled with emotion.

She placed her hand on his arm. "Truly, Matthew, don't hold yourself responsible for what happened to me. I'm a better person now. I'm grateful to you, and I'm grateful to God for taking care of me in spite of myself."

"Bye, Mr. Miller." Dylan looked up at him with his big round eyes.

Matthew ruffled the boy's hair. "If you're ever in Apple Creek, now you know where to find me."

For now, at least.

"Oh, Emma." Sarah rose from her chair and went to embrace her weeping sister. "What is going on? I don't understand."

She knew that a woman expecting a child went through a myriad of emotions, and all would pass eventually. Emma's shoulders shook as she sobbed.

Sarah took her seat, once again, and let Emma sniffle until she was finished. She then went to find her a clean handkerchief. "I don't understand."

What Sarah really wanted to say was, "You have everything you wanted. I don't understand why you're not happy." But she didn't.

"It's Jacob. The real reason we're back here early isn't because I'm having a baby and I miss Mamm. I do, but, well, Jacob lost his job at the factory. I don't know what he did, but we had nowhere else to go. I'm so ashamed. I didn't see any other way to do things."

Sarah thought about that for a moment. "But didn't your district help you when he lost his job? What about getting him another job, somewhere else in Wolfesboro?"

"He tried," Emma sniffled again, "but no one will hire him. The cabinetmaker in Wolfesboro said he is lazy. I think the man might have told someone else, because word got around."

Sarah studied the partially crocheted blanket. "But you are here now, with us. Things can turn around if you have a little patience and faith. I know Mamm is very happy to have you here, and so am I." She realized how feeble the words sounded.

If Jacob was truly lazy and couldn't keep a cabinetmaking job, what would he do when presented with a farm to run?

Although, Sarah considered, maybe he preferred to be outdoors, working with his hands and farming, caring for the animals.

"You're right. I am sure." Emma gave her a smile. "Would you like to see the things I have so far for the baby?"

"Of course I would."

Emma shifted to stand, and it was apparent the weight of the baby was causing her challenges to rise from a seated position. "I can't believe how much longer I still have to go before the baby comes."

They both scaled the stairs and headed for the room the two of them used to share, long ago. Now it was set up for a married couple. A tiny cradle sat in the corner. It was already stacked with blankets. Sarah had made room for them by moving into the smaller room upstairs.

The scene tugged at Sarah's heart. "You've been busy crocheting."

Emma gave a wry smile. "I'm no good at knitting. I would get the house clean and the chores done, and have not much else to do except quilt. That's hard to do alone, you know."

"I know." Sarah nodded. "We're still quilting every week, though. I know it's a sin, but I'm a bit proud that we finished a Light in the Valley quilt a while back, and now we've started another quilt, a Log Cabin in crazy colors. I believe Patience Oberholtz is finishing a rag quilt."

"I miss the weekly get-togethers."

"Well, you'll be welcome the next time we meet."

Emma set down the baby blanket she'd picked up from the cradle, then eased herself down on the mattress, which creaked when she did so.

"What is it?" Although she'd found her sister to be changed, the look of wanting to share something important was the same.

"You're not going to be very happy when I tell you, I think."

"Not happy about what?"

Fresh tears streamed down Emma's cheeks. "I'm reaping what I've sown."

Sarah took a seat on the mattress beside Emma. "Whatever are you talking about?"

Emma wiped her eyes and took a deep breath. Red blotches had formed on her face. "When Jacob and I started courting, it had nothing to do with you, but everything to do with me."

"With you?" Sarah stared at the sampler hanging on the wall.

Emma had stitched it, years ago. "I remember he—Jacob—well, lost interest in me."

"I am surprised no one told you how it happened. It was my fault." Then the story tumbled out as Sarah listened. Emma had been interested in Jacob, but when she saw Sarah had captured his attention, she was jealous.

"Then one night, after he walked you home after a singing, I snuck out and followed him. We'd—we'd been talking here and there. We walked and we talked all night." Emma's shoulders drooped. "But then, we went to the back pasture, to sit and watch the stars, and we fell asleep. I promise, that's all we did. I tried to sneak in the house the next morning, but Daed was there already, waiting. So then he talked to Bishop and the other elders, and Jacob was told to court me."

Sarah sat on the edge of the bed. She could scarcely breathe, and she didn't know what to feel. It answered a big question she'd never had answered, until now.

In seeing her sister and Jacob together, she felt rather relieved that he hadn't chosen her after all. He was rather silly for a grown man. He liked to write, which was not a bad thing, but one couldn't support a family by writing for *The Budget*.

"That's why I feel like I've reaped what I've sown."

"How so?"

"I think . . . I think he snuck out of the house one night, before we left Wolfesboro."

Ah, so there it was. She was suspicious of Jacob. "Did you ask him about it?"

"He said he couldn't sleep and went for a long walk in the fields. It's probably because of his job. But I don't like that he's unhappy."

Sarah nodded. "I see. Well, Jacob and I were not betrothed when he, ah, changed his mind. Yes, it did hurt. I didn't understand, but now I do, and I'm not angry with either one of you. I'm glad you told me."

"Maybe that's what's been bothering me. I could not be under the same roof as you if you didn't know. Because you're my sister."

At that, Sarah hugged her. Yes, it had been a selfish thing and years ago, but looking back, Sarah was thankful that her prayer to marry Jacob Plank had gone unanswered. But now, she worried about her sister and wondered what she could do to help her.

13

Matthew collected eight eggs that morning, enough for breakfast for the next couple of days. If they had more than they needed, he'd take them over to the Stoltzfuses, whose household had increased in size.

The sound of buggy wheels on gravel sounded, and Matthew brought his basket out into the farmyard. It was Bishop Hilty, Levi Stoltzfus, and Herbert Byler. What was the purpose of *this* visit? Bishop wore a grim face as he pulled the buggy to a halt.

The three stepped down, their strides purposeful as they headed in Matthew's direction.

"Good morning, Matthew," Bishop Hilty called.

He couldn't think of anything that warranted a visit from not only the bishop, but two of the elders in the district.

Had something happened to Abraham? His uncle had traveled, by hired car, for a doctor's appointment—this one to prove to everyone that he was in good enough health to travel to Florida.

"There is a serious matter, which we need to discuss." Bishop Hilty dispensed with any niceties.

"All right," Matthew replied. "I will put these eggs away, then join you on the porch."

Bishop nodded. "We'll be here, outside."

Heart pounding in his chest, Matthew carried the basket inside and set it on the kitchen table. He rejoined them on the porch as soon as he could.

"Please sit down." He motioned to the chairs on the porch and a low bench. He decided to lean on the railing. There was no way he could have sat down to listen. He would have fidgeted worse than a five-year-old. Something was wrong. Really wrong.

Bishop glanced at his companions before speaking. Herbert looked sympathetic and Levi looked disgruntled. The bishop? Matthew couldn't gauge the man's expression.

"To get right to it, some serious concerns have been brought to us, both by members here and in the Wolfesboro district." Bishop paused, stroking his beard. "I realize that when a young person takes part in Rumspringa, there are certain things which may occur and certain activities in which they might take part."

Matthew nodded. Not every youth participated in the tradition, or the sowing of wild oats, however one thought of it.

"There are some very serious allegations about a former relationship of yours, and questions about a young child named Dylan Mast."

Matthew closed his eyes. So that was it. Tongues had wagged and assumptions had been made. He had to put the rumors to rest and quickly.

"While we can't condemn anything that was done during Rumspringa, we want to know if this is true, and if it is, that you are taking responsibility for this child."

Matthew looked the bishop in the eye and stood tall. "Rebecca Mast left the community with me, years ago. We were close friends—I considered her my girlfriend. But we did not ever have the kind of relationship you are alluding to. We parted ways not a year after we left Wolfesboro, and I never saw her again until she came by here to see me. We talked about the past. She's doing well. Dylan is a boy she adopted. He is not her biological child."

All three men stared at Matthew, clearly trying to gauge his candor.

He stood his ground. "Anyone who had questions was free to ask me, rather than gossip about something they know nothing about."

Herbert stood. "Now, now. Why does Matthew need to prove any of this?" He waved his arms. "This is ridiculous. I'm going to wait in the buggy." Herbert shook his head as he stomped away from the steps.

"Well?" Bishop asked. "Do you have anything else to say?"

Matthew crossed his arms over his chest. "I have nothing to hide. If that child were mine, I would support him. And I am very disappointed to think that you don't believe Rebecca—a woman who lost her way for a while but has now turned her life around with God's help—and that you don't believe me. Have a good day."

He entered the house, letting the screen door shut with a bang of its own accord. Maybe he'd just sealed the deal and ruined his chances of being accepted into the district. At the moment, he didn't care.

He sat on a chair and watched from the window until they left. He needed to get out, to think. If he'd been back in the English world, he would have taken a ride in his car. Here? Well, he'd take a ride in the buggy until he was ready to come home. But this place was looking less and less like home by the moment.

Sarah hummed happily. The shadows had grown longer, the sun's glare lessened. The traffic of customers was increasing now that it was autumn, not that she minded one bit. The farm stand's coffers would be brimming, and she and Katelynn were going to end the year on a very good note indeed.

Things were better than ever between her and Emma. And now that her old question about Jacob was answered and that was all laid to rest, she felt freer than she had in a long time. It didn't bother her at all now that the two of them lived with her under the same roof. If it bothered Emma and Jacob, neither of them showed it.

The Miller farm would soon belong to the Stoltzfuses, thanks to the agreement that had been signed. Soon Emma would set up house next door.

She didn't know what that meant for Matthew. Where would he live after the house was sold? She couldn't see him staying on there at the farm as a hired hand for Jacob and Emma. Another family, an older couple perhaps, might let him stay in exchange for helping with chores and maintenance of their property. It was hard not to worry about him. But she knew Gött's will would prevail, and whatever that would be, she knew she needed to accept it.

Katelynn had just left for the bank to get more change—they'd had a busy morning, and everyone seemed to be paying with large bills. She also said she'd pick up some more pumpkins as the first load she'd brought earlier had already sold.

A vehicle pulled up, a familiar one. Keith Donnelly was driving.

Ever since the day she and Katelynn had canned the apple butter and discussed their plans for Thanksgiving pies, Keith had seemed a bit friendlier and less creepy, to use a word from Katelynn's vocabulary.

"Hey, Sarah." He strode toward the farm stand. His forehead was covered in sweat and his hands shook.

"Hello. Katelynn will be back very soon. If you'd like to wait here, you can."

He blinked rapidly. "Look, can you do me a favor? I'm a bit short on cash at the moment. I only need fifty dollars."

"That's quite a bit of money. Maybe we should wait to ask Katelynn when she gets back." Even if she was inclined to give him money—which she most certainly was not—it wouldn't be proper to raid the till with Katelynn not there to agree to it.

All of Katelynn's old warnings about Keith rushed into her mind. Sarah's heartbeat increased its pace.

Keith licked his lips as he stared at the barn. "I'm sure she's okay with it, really. Just give me the money."

Sarah stared at him. There was something wrong with the man, but it wasn't clear just what.

"Do you want some water? You don't look as if you feel well." She started to head for the small cooler inside the stand, but Keith grabbed her arm.

"I don't want water. I need money."

She pulled away from him. "Stop. You're scaring me."

"C'mon." He took a deep breath. "It's all right. I'm not trying to scare you. I just. Need. Money. Shoot, I'll even write an IOU." He glanced toward the counter where they bagged purchases. "Got a pencil and paper? I'll do it right now, to show you I mean it. I'm good for it."

Sarah stalled for time. If only she had a cell phone, she could call Katelynn and tell her to hurry. Or Katelynn could at least talk to her brother and see what was the matter.

He began to pace, stomping back and forth outside of the farm stand. "Where is your money box? Just open it and give me something. Anything. C'mon. You don't know what it's like. I need a drink."

Sarah stayed still, not wanting him to know the box had been upgraded and moved. It didn't work. He stepped into the stand, then reached behind the counter.

"Here it is." He tried to open it, the newer, more secure box. "Where's the key?" The young man reeked of alcohol.

"I think you should call a doctor. You don't look like you're feeling well." She reached for the box. "Please, give me the box. We'll wait for Katelynn."

He pulled it back from her. The sound of hooves made them both look up.

While he was distracted, Sarah made her move, lunging for the box.

"No!" Keith snatched it back, then gave her a shove.

Sarah's arms failed as she lost her footing, then she felt a white-hot crack of pain when she hit something sharp.

14

Matthew saw an English man yank something away from Sarah, then shove her backward. She slipped, her head striking the corner of the farm stand's framing, then bouncing forward as her body shot forward.

Rage coursed through Matthew and he urged the horses forward the rest of the way, then leaped from the wagon.

"How dare you!" Matthew bellowed, yanking the man by the neck of his T-shirt.

"Hey, man, hands off." He shoved Matthew away. "It was an accident."

"Not quite." Without another thought, Matthew's fist seemed to ball up of its own accord.

"What are you going to do, hit me?" The man stepped up so that he was nearly nose to nose with Matthew, who tried to keep his composure.

"What did you do to her?"

"C'mon, big guy, I know you wanna hit me. One punch. Just get it out of your system." The guy stepped back, gesturing toward his chest as he did so.

Matthew clenched his teeth, but he wouldn't give in. "No."

The man lashed out at him and Matthew sidestepped nimbly. The punch intended for Matthew swung wide and landed on the edge of the farm stand's outdoor shelf.

Off-balance, the man slipped and his forehead clipped the shelf as well. He collapsed to the dirt and cursed as he did so, clutching his forehead.

Then he was back to his feet and came at Matthew. He swung again, while Matthew ducked.

Matthew looked to Sarah, and it immediately snapped his focus from the man. Blood bloomed from her head and onto the dirt road.

"Sarah!" He flew to her side, kneeling on the ground. Should he move her? His mind tried to think of what to do. *Stop the bleeding.*

"Call 911. Now!" he shouted, this time at this maniac.

"Oh, I've already called them." Keith's voice shook. "Ma'am," he said into the phone, "please send an ambulance and the sheriff to Apple Creek Road. There's a young woman here. Hurt. Blood. And I've been attacked."

Matthew ripped his outer shirt off. Thankfully, he'd worn an undershirt today. He balled the shirt up and compressed it to Sarah's head. Her eyes were closed. He felt her neck. Yes, she breathed. But there was so much blood.

A feminine scream came from the direction of the house. Emma. She came running.

"What have you done?" She skittered to a stop, clamped one hand over her mouth, then ran toward the barn. "*Daed!*"

Meanwhile, the man paced back and forth, as if unsure of what to do. A familiar truck approached the farm stand. That would be Katelynn, Sarah's friend.

"What on earth?" Katelynn said as she jumped from the driver's seat of the truck. "Keith, did you have something to do with this?"

Matthew tried not to glare at him, instead praying silently that Sarah would wake up, that the bleeding would stop.

"It was an accident. I pushed her away, and she fell." Keith rubbed his head. "I wasn't trying to hurt her."

Matthew ventured a glance at the man. On his forehead bloomed a thin red line of blood.

"But that—that Amish man there attacked me!"

"What?" Katelynn stared at Matthew, her mouth agape.

"I did no such thing."

The unmistakable wail of sirens sounded in the distance. Matthew's silent prayer continued; this time it was one of thanks that help was coming soon. He knew that going to the English for help wasn't their way, not most of the time. But he wanted expert care for Sarah. And if she needed to go to the hospital, he would make sure she got there.

Sarah's Mamm ran from the house. She knelt on the other side of her daughter. "Danke, Matthew."

Lights flashed in the sunlight, lights from an ambulance and from a patrol car that now blocked all vehicles—horse-drawn and otherwise—at the farm stand.

Matthew stood to make way for the emergency responders to do their work. He turned to face an officer that had left the patrol car.

"There he is." Keith pointed at Matthew. "There's the man who punched me. He attacked me. And I want to press charges." His voice shook.

Matthew worried that his explanation would sound feeble. Part of him had wanted to punch Keith, but that wasn't the same as actually doing it. He could only hope the police would believe him over this obviously impaired man.

Sarah was having a dream, and it was a bad one. A wailing horn, lights flashing, all adding to the searing pain in her head. She fought to breathe, fought to open her eyes. Then darkness came again, and voices around her talked about things that didn't register.

Her eyes fluttered open, and she saw she wasn't in her room, but in a cold, sharp-smelling place with lights and machines. She wanted to cry, she wanted her Mamm as if she were a little child again. Then it was quiet, and she stopped dreaming and opened her eyes.

"She's awake!" Her mother's voice sounded above a repeating beep.

Everything hurt. She tried to move, felt a bed railing beneath the fingers of her right hand as the ceiling swam into focus. A light was on somewhere behind her head and cast a soft glow over her.

She realized she was in an English hospital room. The walls were gray, a soft gray like a dove, and the room's white curtains blocked enough of the light that Sarah couldn't figure out if it was day or night.

Her Mamm rose from a nearby chair and clasped Sarah's hands between her own callused ones. "We prayed and prayed. Gött has heard us."

Emma joined their mother at the bedside. "Oh, Sarah. It's been just horrible. The sheriff came, and—"

Mamm silenced Emma with a look.

Sarah's head hurt. She felt a dull ache all over. "Sheriff?"

"We'll talk about *that* later," Mamm said. "You took a fall, a bad one."

"I was at the farm stand." Sarah closed her eyes. It was time to take pie orders. She'd made a sign, and both she and Katelynn had been busy that morning. Katelynn had gone to the bank to get change.

"Do you remember . . . what happened?" Her mother's brows furrowed, the shadows beneath her eyes deepening in the low light of the room.

"I guess I fell? But I'm not sure how. Katelynn was gone." Her stomach growled. "I'm hungry."

At that, the door creaked open, and the light and bustle from the hall outside entered the room along with a shadowed figure. It was an English woman, wearing a pink cotton shirt and pink pants. The shirt had cats printed all over it. Even in her befuddled state, Sarah stared at the vivid clothing as its wearer came closer to the bed.

The woman, not much older than Sarah, smiled down at her. "Sarah, how are you feeling?"

Mamm and Emma made way for the nurse, who studied the machines on the pole beside the bed.

"My head hurts some. My back hurts too." She tried to think. What had happened?

"That's understandable. The doctor will stop by soon, and we'll see about getting you discharged tonight, we hope."

How long had she been here? She said nothing as the nurse made some notes.

"I've put in for a lunch tray for you, and we'll see how that goes. Are you hungry at all?"

"I am." Sarah nodded.

They talked about her pain level, and the nurse removed the plastic tubing that connected to something stuck into her wrist that was covered with fabric tape. Only then did Sarah notice that her hand ached a little where the device had been.

The nurse left, the door clicking shut gently behind her.

Mamm glanced over her shoulder before speaking. "You've been here since yesterday."

"I remember a little more now." She recalled a fitful sleep, which she thought had been a dream itself. Voices and shadows intermittent with bright lights.

"Your head just wouldn't stop bleeding." Emma's voice shook. "We were so scared. I never prayed so hard, not ever."

"What about the farm stand? Does Katelynn know?"

"Jah, she knows." Mamm shook her head. "She is coming here today. She was here last night, but then left."

"What aren't you telling me?"

Another knock at the door, and in came a trio of people—the bishop and his wife, and Jeremiah, who looked a bit nervous, hanging back behind his aunt and uncle.

"We hope now is a good time to visit," said Louisa. "Are you better, I hope and pray?"

"Better," was all Sarah knew to say at the moment. Her Mamm frowned and Emma wore the same expression.

"What happened was inexcusable," said the bishop.

"Now is not the time." The bishop might be head of the district, but his wife was known to step in and speak her mind.

Jeremiah said nothing, but even in the soft light Sarah could see the concern in his eyes as he looked at her. He seemed a kind young man, and she did like him, what little she knew of him. But why was he here? Not that it mattered.

She wanted to see Matthew and wanted to ask her Mamm about him, but she decided with the Hiltys present, it wasn't the best idea.

Louisa cleared her throat before continuing. "You have been in all our prayers. We were here, today, visiting another of our sick, so thought it good to see you too."

"Thank you, all, very much, for coming to see me."

"They think she might go home today," Mamm interjected.

"Will you need a driver? There is room in the van, I believe," said the bishop.

"Oh, that would be very good if there was room. But we wouldn't want to keep you waiting." Mamm nodded as she spoke.

Sarah closed her eyes, letting them discuss the possible traveling arrangements. The subject of coffee came up among the three eldest, who decided to go to the hospital cafeteria and also consult with the driver by telephone about the return to Apple Creek.

"We will be back," Mamm said. She and the bishop and Mrs. Hilty moved to leave, but Jeremiah and Emma remained. Emma gave Jeremiah a suspicious glance as she took a seat in the corner of the room.

That left Jeremiah with the only other chair in the room, adjacent to Sarah's bed.

"May I sit down?" He motioned to the chair.

"Jah, of course." She nodded, the movement causing a slight ache in her head.

"My aunt and uncle were very worried about you." Jeremiah's voice had a warm, comforting tone. "But I knew God would take care of you and His will would be done."

"I'm glad you knew that. But I remember nothing of what happened. Not really." Again her mind struggled to link together the chain of events.

Emma shook her head. "Oh, Sarah. Mamm didn't want me to say, but Matthew was taken away by the sheriff."

15

The events of the last twenty-four hours were something out of a bad dream. Matthew used to have bad dreams when he was out among the English, but nothing like this.

Nothing like the real-life scenario that had unfolded. The fields passed by as he rode inside a McNairy County deputy's patrol car—this time in the front seat and not in the back, where he'd ridden in handcuffs yesterday to the county jail where he'd spent the night.

His shoulders drooped, even as the deputy kept up pleasant conversation, talking about horses and farming.

"You've been released on your personal recognizance, Mr. Miller," the judge had told him not quite two hours earlier. "Do you understand what that means?"

He did. He'd lived in the English world long enough to know basic police terminology.

"It means I promise I will stay out of trouble—and away from Keith Donnelly—until it is time for court," he'd told the judge.

"You'll receive a notice from the court for a hearing date."

With that, he'd been dismissed and was free to go. The deputy, about his age, offered to give him a ride home to the farm because he was on his way home anyway. It wasn't like Matthew could call anyone to come and get him. And even if he could—and even though he was innocent—the shame he felt would have precluded him from making contact with anyone in the community

"My granddaddy had a place out near yours," the deputy was

saying. "We used to go out there when I was a kid, run the fields and watch the buggies go by."

Matthew struggled to make conversation. "Yes, there's an English family, a few farms over. I don't know them. I haven't been here long. I've been living with my father's older brother to help him on the farm."

"Yeah, it's hard, watching someone getting up there in years. I'm glad one of my uncles moved in with my grandfather and took over the farm. Hard work, running a farm. I always knew I wanted to be an officer of the law. But we're happy the farm has stayed in the family."

The deputy turned the corner onto the country road, and Matthew could see the green spot in the distance that was the mailbox that belonged to the Miller farm.

The deputy pulled into the driveway. "Your uncle at home, you think?"

"Yes. It's about suppertime, and he wouldn't be gone after dark."

The patrol car continued along the driveway, but Deputy Dickey had to put on the brakes before reaching the farmyard. A row of buggies lined the driveway and effectively blocked the rest of their journey.

"Looks like this is the end of the line," the deputy said.

"Looks like it." Matthew glanced at the man. If things had been different, he imagined the two of them might have been friends. He liked his easy, kind demeanor.

"Well, you take care." The deputy's brow furrowed. "And hey—I know you were in a tussle with that guy. Don't let it get you down. You've never been in trouble with the law before, so you'll probably just get a warning if there were no marks on the guy and it was just your word against his. Just don't forget to show up for court. If you need legal help, you can get a court-appointed lawyer."

"Thanks." Matthew gave him a nod and left the vehicle.

He turned and watched as the patrol car headed back down the driveway and disappeared. End of the line, huh? As Matthew surveyed the buggies lined up at the fence, he wondered if it was the end of the line for him in more ways than one.

Matthew's boots sounded unnaturally loud on the porch steps when he reached them. He took a deep breath, then entered the house.

Bishop Hilty, his nephew Jeremiah, along with Herbert Byler and other men of the community sat in the living room, along with Abraham. They made a semicircle and all turned to him where he stood.

Abraham's face seemed to have more wrinkles than Matthew remembered, the man's shoulders more hunched. It might as well have been eight months he'd been away, rather than a day and a night.

They all stared at him, and he had no idea of what to say, nor what the situation was in front of him. Clearly, he'd done wrong. He would need to make apologies, all around, for his behavior, though he'd do it again if it meant keeping Sarah safe.

He was desperate to know what had happened to her after the ambulance had left, but of course no one had told him and he'd had no way to find out.

"You're home." Abraham rose from his seat, crossed the room, and embraced Matthew. "You're all right."

Matthew's throat caught as he tried to speak. "Yes, I am. I'm all right."

The older man released him, then took his seat again. "Sit down, Matthew. We need to talk."

Bishop moved as if to speak, but Abraham raised his hand. Surprisingly, the bishop remained silent.

Only one seat remained, an empty chair from the kitchen table. Evidently they'd put out more chairs than needed, or this chair was reserved especially for him.

"What happened, Matthew?" Abraham asked. "We are hearing

several stories, all slightly different tales. But God knows the truth, sees and saw all."

Matthew sat down on the wooden chair. "Yes, He does."

He looked around the room at all of them. It was a very serious thing to strike a person or commit another act of physical violence. But he hadn't done that. He took another deep breath before continuing.

"I left the house yesterday, and as I was passing Sarah Stoltzfus's farm stand, I saw her with Keith Donnelly. I saw them struggle over something, then he pushed her back and she fell." He paused, inhaled deeply again. "So I stopped, then walked up and he tried to punch me. Twice. But I didn't strike him."

He closed his eyes, bowed his head. It sounded so matter-of-fact. But that's exactly what had happened. He dared not say how angry he was about the farm being sold out from under him, about not knowing where he was going, nor about his feelings for Sarah which complicated it all further.

"So you're not the one who pushed her?" Herbert Byler asked.

"Her?" The thought horrified him. "No, Herbert. I did not, nor would I ever do such a thing. How is she? Does anyone know?" Matthew glanced around the room as he spoke. "Please, tell me she will be all right."

The bishop and his nephew exchanged glances. Bishop spoke. "She is going to be all right. Her family has been with her and they believe she will be released today."

Matthew felt an unspeakable relief wash over him. Not much else mattered as much at the moment, now that he knew she was going to be all right.

"We don't know what happened with the English man," the bishop continued, "but our visit right now was to talk with your uncle about what happened. You are in his household, and though it be the two of you and you are a grown man, he is responsible for you."

Matthew shook his head. "I am responsible for my own actions. But I didn't hit him, although I admit I was angry and wanted to. He was taunting me. Goading me."

"What charges do you face with the English?" the bishop asked.

"Assault. Keith told the sheriff's deputy that I struck him, which isn't true. He also said I was the one who pushed her—by accident, but he claims I was the cause of the entire situation." Matthew rubbed his chin. "But that's a lie. And only the three of us were there to witness it. Her mother and sister came out to help—then the ambulance and deputy arrived, and before I knew it, I was being taken away."

He felt as if he were making excuses.

"Keith Donnelly, though," Matthew said aloud again, "he smelled of alcohol, and he was not in his right mind because of it. He was out of control, not making sense."

"I believe you," Herbert said, nodding. "During the time you've been here in our community you have not shown signs of a hasty temper from what I have seen, and your uncle also vouches for you."

"I am sorry for bringing shame to our community. If this causes harm to us, I don't know what I'll do." Matthew frowned at the floor. He knew the incident was likely to make the local newspaper, possibly even television.

"As for the young man, his sister took him away," the bishop said. "I am not sure what became of him, but from what I understand it was to get him medical attention as well."

The weight of the air in the room pressed against Matthew. "Again, I am sorry. At the first opportunity, I will find him, and speak to him and apologize for the argument." He paused, remembering the judge's instructions. "That is, if I am allowed to see him in person to do so."

He glanced at each of their faces before he spoke. He might as well tackle the elephant in the room. "Bishop, if you and the others believe I'm not fit to officially join the church here, I understand."

"That is not our largest concern," said the bishop. "I don't know if you are ready yet. My biggest concern for you, for all of us here, is our eternal souls."

Matthew nodded. "Yes, I understand and appreciate that."

"However," the bishop continued, "I worry about what consequences this incident and the other matter will have when taken together."

"What other matter?" Matthew asked, but part of him already knew the next words.

"The matter of Rebecca Mast. Tongues are still wagging."

Despite his present situation, Matthew couldn't help the anger that reignited inside him about Rebecca. "Both I and Rebecca have shared the truth, that her son is not mine. He is adopted. This has not been hidden. And yet, since you are concerned for all of our souls, you might do well to have a discussion with the gossips who continue to speak as if they know the truth, which is not truth at all. I hope you'll pay them a visit."

He'd had enough. He headed for the steps and took them two at a time upstairs.

Sarah tried not to look for the puddle of dried blood at the edge of the driveway, but still her gaze drifted in that direction as the buggy swayed gently beneath her. There was no blood. Someone must have covered it up with dirt that still made a telltale oddly shaped lump.

After the buggy creaked to a halt, Emma came out to meet her and hugged her close as soon as she stepped from the buggy. "Ach, you're home! It wasn't the same without you here, even for one night."

"Danke, it's good to be home." She glanced at Daed, who'd said little on the drive from the general store, where the hired car had met him driving the buggy.

"Take care you don't squeeze the breath out of your sister," Mamm said from behind Emma. "Inside you go to rest like the doctor said."

"Yes, Mamm." There was a tiny prickle of pain on the back of Sarah's head as she looked up at her home. She'd never spent a night away from it, not in all her years. Today, it felt as though she'd been gone days and days.

Daed carried the bag that contained her soiled clothing, which Mamm took from him to wash later. He hopped back into the buggy and headed for the barn.

Sarah continued with her mother and sister into the house. Jacob, she guessed, was already scouting the land at his and Emma's soon-to-be new home.

"I told Katelynn you would be home this evening," Mamm said. "She has been very worried about you."

"I need to speak with her soon." Sarah nodded. "Her brother, Keith—"

She paused in the doorway and glanced over her shoulder toward the driveway and the farm stand beyond. Keith Donnelly had been there yesterday. No one would tell her, not in a straight story anyway, about what exactly had happened, because, from what she understood, there were several different tellings of the story—and none of them from the two other people who had been there.

Matthew. Her mind replayed a shadowy vision. She was lying on the ground and his face shimmered above her, his face etched with a combination of concern and anger.

"Sarah, are you all right?" Mamm's voice jolted Sarah's focus back to where she stood, clutching the doorframe.

"Jah, for a moment . . ." Her voice trailed off, and she shook her head.

"Come, we will help you upstairs to your room." Mamm gently grasped Sarah's elbow.

"I can do it, Mamm. Danke." She began scaling the steps to the second floor. Emma followed like a shadow, not resting after all, as Mamm had instructed her. Sarah would have preferred to be left alone at the moment, after the nonstop trail of nurses and doctors passing in and out of her hospital room. But she didn't tell Emma that.

No sooner did Sarah get settled beneath her quilt after Emma propped up the pillows on her bed than Emma launched into a story of all Sarah had missed.

"And we will be moving soon, very soon, into our new home." Emma's cheeks flushed, both from the new life within her along with her excitement about the farm.

"Jacob has shown such a new zeal for taking over the farm." Emma sat on the foot of the bed, with her voice taking on a dreamy tone. "I've never seen him show such purpose and determination."

"I'm glad for both of you."

"We are moving in, within the week."

"That is very soon."

Emma nodded. "Jah, it is. But we found out yesterday that Abraham Miller is ready to close on the property, sooner rather than later. His brother is insisting he move to live with him, only until the weather turns and then Abraham will go to Florida."

"And what about Matthew?" She had to know. What would become of him?

"He is moving in with the Bylers."

He wasn't leaving. Her heart squeezed. "I see. Well, Herbert and his wife will certainly welcome the help."

"Jah, I imagine." Then Emma frowned.

"What is it? What aren't you telling me?" Sarah sighed. "Everyone has stepped around the whole story about how I struck my head."

"You really don't remember?"

"Not exactly. Something about him and Keith."

"He and Keith got into a fight about you."

"Me?"

"I'm not sure of what happened, exactly, but Keith said that Matthew knocked you down, accidentally, and then tried to blame him for it and hit him too."

"*Matthew* hit Keith?" Sarah pulled the quilt closer to her chin. "I don't want to believe it. And I don't remember him knocking me down, accidentally or otherwise. He would never do that. Never."

"Someone said that all that time among the English affected him."

"Of course it did. How could it not?"

Emma sank onto the edge of Sarah's bed. "I do feel bad for him. He has worked hard and tried to be accepted here, and it hasn't been easy. He and Jacob don't seem to particularly care for each other, although I can't imagine why."

Sarah could. Matthew had a protective streak, and if he thought Jacob had hurt her, that could certainly account for a bit of bad feeling. It wasn't prideful to think that, was it? She cleared her throat. "Well, I appreciate him standing up for me. No, I don't approve of violence, not at all. But it is comforting to feel that someone would risk his own safety for me." That had to have been what happened. She knew in her heart that Matthew was not a violent man.

"Sarah!" A voice called from downstairs, followed by pounding feet. Lydia entered the room and raced to the edge of Sarah's bed. "Your Mamm said you were home."

At that, the two friends embraced.

"We've been worried, and praying so hard, and we're so thankful you're all right." Lydia tucked the blanket back around her friend. "I didn't believe for a minute Matthew would try to hurt you, and if he did hit that man, there had to have been a pretty good reason for it."

Sarah smiled at both her sister and her friend. "Well, I'm here again, and I'm very thankful. I didn't sleep so well in that hospital. It wasn't like home, not at all."

"Do you need anything?" Emma asked, shifting herself to a stand, her belly now pulling against the skirt of her dress.

"No, I'm happy to just rest for now." Sarah watched as Emma left the room, then turned her focus back to Lydia. "I'm glad you're here."

"Oh, I wish I wasn't visiting you like this, not for this reason, anyway." In spite of her furrowed brow, Lydia looked as if she harbored a secret.

"What is it? Tell me something happy. People keep telling me how worried they've been, and I appreciate their concern, but tell me something else."

Lydia clapped her hands once. "Thad spoke to my father. I'm getting married!"

"Oh!" Sarah blurted out. "But you haven't been courting that long."

"I know, that's what my Mamm said. But Thad and I have known each other for the longest time, and we just, well, we just *know* we should get married. He has big plans, and I love that about him. We've already written our announcement for *The Budget*."

Lydia's enthusiastic story tumbled out, about Thad's idea for a furniture store—in town, not at the family farm—and how they would build their own home on his family's property along with a workshop. She would work at the store.

"I'm so happy for you." Sarah grinned. Lydia's exuberance was always infectious, in a good way. "I know you will do an excellent job working at the store. You like to talk."

At that, Lydia gave a merry laugh and Sarah felt a thousand times better than she had when she'd first returned. She wanted life to be *normal* again, without talk of arguments and fists flying, and who was to blame for what.

"I was thinking, in the spring when we open the store, it might be good to have some quilts on display for sale too."

"Quilts at a furniture store? Why not, especially if you are selling beds."

"It was my idea. But Thad agreed. Our dreams, well, they seem to be very similar, or close enough that we will build them together, with God's help."

Sarah nodded. "That's very sweet, and I'm happy for the two of you."

"Of course, I want you to stand with me. I'm not sure who Thad will ask. But there will be a lot to do and what fun it will be, doing it! Dresses to sew, a meal to plan . . ." Her voice trailed off with a happy sigh.

"Moving, weddings, babies, and some people think nothing happens in a small Amish community," Sarah observed. "There's certainly plenty going on."

"What about you? Will you still sell your pies? I will probably buy a few myself so I don't have to bake for Thanksgiving. Mamm asked me to make the desserts this year, but she probably wouldn't mind me buying them from you."

"I haven't talked to Katelynn yet, but that's what I'd like to do. I know after a day or two of rest here, I'll be ready to get back to work again."

"I don't know about that," said a voice in the doorway. Mamm had come to check on her. "I've already cleared what's left in your garden and sold some of it. But don't push yourself to bake the pies if you're not up to it."

"I already accepted payment for thirteen orders. I don't want to cancel on them."

Mamm nodded. "All right, if you and your friend need help, you know I'll do my best."

"Me too," Lydia said. "And I'll even pay for my own."

Sarah chuckled at her friend. She was so grateful to be back home.

But there was one person she wanted to see, more than anyone else. Matthew. And she knew exactly what she needed to do, to thank him properly for wanting to protect her.

16

Matthew pulled the zipper to open his suitcase and looked around the simple, comfortable room. There hadn't been much to bring with him when he'd left Abraham's home—what was now Jacob Plank's home. Herbert had been adamant about Matthew coming to stay with them "until everything else has been settled."

He strode to the window and looked out at the field, now cleared after the harvest. The Bylers had grown children to help them, if need be. A son lived less than three miles away, and more sons lived in Wolfesboro.

Nobody really needed him here in Apple Creek, not anymore.

The sound of footsteps outside the open bedroom door made him turn around. Herbert stood in the doorway. He stretched his suspenders with his thumbs.

"*Gut*, you are unpacking. Lavinia will have supper on the table by five. First thing tomorrow, I will show you a few of the things that can be done around here."

"Danke, Herbert."

"We are glad you're here."

"And I am glad to be here." Matthew pulled his extra pairs of trousers from the suitcase and placed them in the chest of drawers.

"I hope this home will be a place where you will come to know the direction God intends for your life," said Herbert. "I am going to the general store to pick up the box of nails that we will need tomorrow. Would you like to come as well?"

"Jah, I would." He'd been in a slump since his encounter with Keith Donnelly. For the most recent Sunday gathering, he had stayed home alone. Maybe the trip to town would do him some good.

They made quick time to the general store, and Herbert went directly to the store's small yet varied hardware section.

Meanwhile, Matthew stared at the public phone, one of the throwbacks to earlier days of the English. Most English had cell phones now. During his years outside the Amish community, he'd had a phone he carried everywhere with him. Now he didn't miss it so much.

Now would be as good a time as any to call his parents and leave a message for them at the phone shanty near their farm. He wasn't sure if anyone would answer, but there was voice mail and he could leave a message.

"Do you need to make a call, sir?" asked the young man behind the counter. "It's free, but don't be on more than five minutes or so."

Matthew nodded. "Yes. I . . . I won't take long." He pulled out his wallet and retrieved the folded slip of paper inside on which he'd written the number before he left Wolfesboro. He hadn't called them previously but had responded to several letters from his Mamm.

He hadn't written them about the incident, although it had been a week since it occurred. Since people went back and forth between Wolfesboro and Apple Creek, there was a good chance they already knew.

"You can talk in the storage room if you need a little privacy." The kid nodded toward a doorway in the opposite wall.

"Thank you." Matthew took the cordless receiver, then stepped into the room before punching in the numbers. It rang several times and just before he expected the connection to click over to voice mail, another click sounded instead.

"Jah? This is Judith Miller."

Matthew's throat caught at the sound of her voice. "Mamm."

"Ach, Matthew. I was walking by, on my way back to the house after picking up our mail. Why are you calling?"

"I, ah. I wanted to say hello and see how you and Daed are doing."

Her voice was warm, with a lilt. "We are both well. Your Daed is seeing to the team and working on the harness before supper today."

"That's *gut*." He wiped one of his sweaty palms on his trouser leg. "I am staying with Herbert and Lavinia Byler now, though I'm sure Abraham told you. How is he?"

"He is his usual self, though I have never seen him so excited. I am not sure him going to Florida will be wise, so far from most of his family."

"It was hard for him to decide to sell, so it would be hard to convince him to stay here, in Tennessee." Matthew glanced toward the sales counter area. Herbert held a box of nails. The older man scratched his chin as he looked at the assortment of chocolate bars at the counter.

"Son, there's something in your voice. What is it? A Mamm never forgets the sound of her child's worried voice."

Matthew closed his eyes. "Is there a chance I might come back to Wolfesboro, to see if the cabinet or furniture shop is hiring?"

"We always have room for you." Her voice was warm.

"Danke, Mamm. I am not sure yet about when. But I will let you know as soon as I decide."

"Your Daed won't admit it, but he would welcome the help here too. There's always something to be done."

"Danke again, Mamm."

"Of course. We will talk soon. Goodbye."

The connection went silent and Matthew pushed the button on the phone, which he returned to the clerk after leaving the storage room.

"You done?" Herbert asked as Matthew rounded the other side of the counter.

"Jah. Called my Mamm."

The clerk totaled up Herbert's purchases, for which Herbert fished some bills out of his wallet.

"*Gut.* You told them you're staying with us for now?"

Matthew nodded. They said goodbye to the clerk, then left the store.

As the two of them stepped from the porch, where Herbert looked wistfully at the empty chairs on opposite sides of the checkerboard, another buggy approached. Levi was at the reins.

The man's brow furrowed when he caught sight of Matthew walking to the buggy with Herbert. Matthew looked away. He hadn't spoken to Levi since shortly after the incident, upon Sarah's arrival home. Even when he tried to find the right words to say, an attempt at conversation hadn't gone well.

Levi reined the horse to a halt and lost no time tying it to the hitching post at the side of the parking lot. Matthew stood quietly by while Herbert untied his own horse's reins from the post.

"Hello, Levi," Matthew managed to say.

"Hello." Levi paused between the two buggies. "You are still here, I see."

"Jah. Just on a quick stop by the store before supper." But Levi's tone spoke volumes and had nothing to do with Matthew's presence at the general store.

"I mean, you are still here in Apple Creek." The man took a step forward. "Whether or not you have committed a crime, you have brought trouble here, and it would be wise for you to leave."

"Now, Levi," Herbert began, joining them at the buggy after tossing the reins onto the front seat.

"Now, nothing. There is nothing for you here in Apple Creek."

"You mean Sarah." Matthew tried to keep his voice even. She *was* keeping him here, even though he couldn't court her. Especially not after the incident with Keith Donnelly.

"I mean, you would be better somewhere else. My daughter Sarah knows better. She could be a bishop's wife one day, not the wife of an Englisher who thinks he can be Amish again."

Matthew nodded. "I see. Did Sarah tell you she wants to be a bishop's wife?"

"She deserves to be a bishop's wife. She deserves a man who controls his temper and actions, and does not fill her head with distractions."

"I believe that is something Sarah will decide on her own." Matthew swallowed hard and squared his shoulders. "And I have not approached Sarah to ask to court her anyway."

"Levi," Herbert said. "This is not your conversation to have. You are trying to protect her, jah, but you are also acting as judge. Gött is our judge."

"But if this man thinks he is going to be approved to join our fellowship, he is wrong." Levi pointed at Matthew. "We need to see by his conduct that he is truly one of us, and we do *not* raise our hands to another in anger."

With that, Levi waved both hands and stomped off toward the general store. Matthew watched him go inside before saying anything more.

"He's right, in a way." Matthew relaxed his shoulders. "I wasn't a good example, and now I'm in trouble with the law, even though it wasn't my fault."

"Come." Herbert motioned to the buggy. "Let's go home."

They both climbed aboard. Herbert maneuvered the buggy in the direction of the country road and paused as a truck roared by. The horse's ears merely flicked at the offending sound and rumble of the vehicle.

If only Matthew's own demeanor could be as unflappable toward all the roaring going on inside him and around him. Perhaps it would help to talk to this kind man, his elder.

Once they were on the road to the farm, Matthew said, "I want to apologize to Keith Donnelly in person for the argument, but it was recommended that I not try to contact him at all while the charges are pending. I reacted in anger when I saw him push Sarah, then saw her fall. When I confronted him, we argued. He taunted me, daring me to hit him. But I didn't. He tried to hit me, lost his balance, then slipped and hit his head."

Minutes passed. Why wasn't Herbert saying anything? Herbert reined in the horse at the crossroads and checked both ways before urging the horse forward again.

"There was something wrong with Keith. I think he was having some kind of a mental . . . episode combined with the fact that he was drunk. But he was in a rage for some reason, and I was a ready target." Matthew inhaled deeply and blew out a breath. He didn't think he needed to explain anything more.

"And now you're in trouble with the law, with no one else but you, Sarah, and the young man witnessing what happened, and Sarah not remembering . . ."

"Sarah doesn't remember what happened?" He wasn't sure if that was good or bad. If she couldn't recall his behavior, she couldn't think less of him. But if she could recall the incident, she would rightfully be able to condemn him for not being able to control his temper better. Not that it mattered much. Either way, he couldn't have her.

"No, not completely, from what Levi has said. Another reason he spoke as he did just now. That's his daughter."

"I understand. If someone hurt my daughter, I would have a hard time not feeling angry toward anyone I believed responsible for it . . ."

Matthew's thoughts took over. He desperately wanted to call on Sarah, just to see her once more. To hear her voice. To tell her . . .

He made a decision. The time for hanging his head in shame was over. He'd deal with his legal problems, and when it was appropriate, he would apologize to Keith Donnelly.

Even if there was absolutely no chance of him and Sarah being together, at least he would do the right thing—even if it was the last thing he did before leaving Apple Creek for good.

The ladies gathered at the Stoltzfuses' for their usual quilting on Wednesday morning. Lydia and the others had told Sarah on Sunday that if she wanted to cancel quilting day, they didn't mind one bit.

"Not at all," she'd said. Sarah wanted to get back to her regular activities as soon as she could. The English doctor wanted her to return to the hospital's radiology clinic next week for a scan of her head, just as a precaution. But in the meantime, she wanted to do what she loved—quilting and caring for what was left of her garden. Keeping her hands busy would keep her mind from going to the one place it seemed to settle far too often these days—Matthew.

The new Log Cabin quilt was nearly complete. Today they would finish the corners and then set to work on the binding. Perhaps they didn't need six women to work on it today, but Sarah loved having everyone there and the light chatter flowing around the room.

Emma sat in one corner of the living room, where she continued crocheting. She'd always found quilting tedious, she said, while Sarah felt the same way about working with yarn.

"Thanksgiving is coming," observed Patience Oberholtz. "I say, I do enjoy the meal, but there's always so much to do every year."

Emma spoke up from her corner. "Well, you could always buy some pies from Sarah and her English friend Katelynn."

"You haven't changed your mind about that?" Mamm asked. "No one would blame you, you know, as long as you return the money they paid up front."

Sarah nodded and was pleased to note that her head didn't hurt when she did so. "We are still going to make our pies. I've decided this will be my last season of the farm stand, though I haven't told Katelynn yet."

"Probably for the best, anyway," said Patience. "Englishers and our ways don't mix well. Although, your garden and farm stand have done a great deal of work to raise funds to aid those in need. For that, I know we're all thankful."

"Danke," Sarah said. "I'll keep the garden up next year." However, a knot had formed in her throat at the thought of this Thanksgiving being the last sales from the stand, so to speak. Her last business venture with Katelynn. Ach, things were changing.

She continued to stitch the area in front of her. With the end of each quilt project, there was a sense of accomplishment and a bit of disappointment. After this, what next?

The morning was balmy for November, and the front door was open to let the fresh air blow through the screen door and into the living room. Sarah could hear a vehicle's engine growing louder as it came up the driveway. But the farm stand wasn't really open, nor was the sign up that they had anything for sale today.

Mamm rose from her chair, motioning for Emma to stay seated. Sarah's sister would have had trouble getting up from her seated position, as close as the baby was to coming. "I'll see to whoever it is."

The vehicle's engine stopped as Mamm went to the door and watched. Footsteps grew louder, and then a familiar form stood on the other side of the screen. Katelynn. She clutched something in her hands.

"Please come in," Mamm said, a bit hesitantly.

Katelynn looked apologetic as she scanned the room and saw the women gathered. "I am very sorry for the interruption. Is this a bad time, Sarah, to talk to you for just a few minutes?"

"Of course not." It was then that Sarah noticed Katelynn held the farm stand's cashbox in her hands. "Please, come to the kitchen, and we can talk there."

They settled in the two remaining chairs set up at the table. "You've got the cashbox. Good. I was wondering where it was and hadn't had the chance to ask you about it."

Katelynn nodded. "That's just it. I have the box because it's been at my house. Except I'm not the one who brought it to my house."

Her brain was recovered sufficiently for her to know what that meant. "Keith took it."

Katelynn slid the box across the table to Sarah. As soon as Sarah touched it, everything came back in a flash of memory. Keith. The argument. Him grabbing the box, her trying to get it back from him. The shove and pain. Then shouting of men's voices, and Matthew leaning over her. An ambulance ride.

"Where is Keith?" she managed to ask.

"That's just it . . . I don't know." Katelynn's shoulders sank. "Right after you were hurt, and I took him home—he refused to go to the doctor—he was frantic, talking about the police and everything. But the next morning, he disappeared. He left his things but took his truck."

Sarah nodded slowly. "It was an accident, him pushing me. I don't think he wanted to hurt me, he only wanted the cashbox. But he was acting so strangely, I was really afraid."

Tears formed in Katelynn's eyes. "He's met more of the same kind of people that he got into trouble with before, it seems." Katelynn frowned. "And there's nothing my family can do about it. I'm so sorry, Sarah. My family drama has spilled over into your life. I'll never forgive myself for leaving you alone at the farm stand. Never."

With that, a tear slid down Katelynn's cheek. Sarah reached for a tissue out of the box on the table and handed it to her.

"It wasn't your fault, Katelynn. I could never blame one of my dearest friends."

Katelynn sniffled and looked up at her, then dabbed at her eyes. "You're one of my dearest friends too. He's off his medications. We can't leave cash or valuables in the house. He wanted cash that day, didn't he?"

Sarah nodded. "I remember . . . he was looking for you, but you'd gone to the bank for more change. He was getting very forceful, he looked frantic." She tried not to shudder at the fresh recollection of Keith's voice, his darting eyes, and shaking movements just prior to her fall.

"You were lucky that Matthew came just in time to help you."

"I'm glad he did. It wasn't luck, but God's will that he be there." She sighed, realizing that because of Keith, Matthew's reputation in the community hadn't fared so well.

"I'm floored that Keith pressed charges against him." Katelynn shook her head. "He disappeared before I could talk him out of it. And I really don't know what he told the police about Matthew either. What a mess, and it's all because of Keith. I'm so sorry . . ."

Katelynn reached for a fresh tissue.

"We will pray for your brother that he will make the right choices and do what pleases God. It's not your fault what he's done," she repeated.

"If you don't want to do the pies after all, I'll understand. We can refund customers what we've collected so far."

"No. We'll go forward, this one last time. It's time we close the farm stand."

Katelynn nodded. "I didn't want to tell you, I've been thinking the same thing. With the wedding planning, and this semester, I've felt like this would be a good time to end it. After we bake the pies."

"I agree. Our customers want their Thanksgiving desserts, and we will not disappoint them."

Katelynn wiped her eyes. "Good, then. I'm glad we're on the same page with this. But I'll miss seeing you, after all is said and done."

"Well, you'll be seeing me for another two weeks or so, at least." Sarah stood. "And this doesn't mean we won't see each other again—it'll just be less frequent. Would you like a cup of coffee? Or a pastry? You can come sit with us while we stitch, if you want to."

"I can stay, for a little bit." Katelynn glanced toward the living room. "They won't mind?"

"Of course not. We can also talk about the pies. Maybe we'll get a few orders." She smiled at Katelynn and motioned toward the living room. But she left the cashbox on the table.

Part of her was relieved that she'd remembered, and part of her was horrified at what Keith had done to Matthew, especially getting the English law involved.

But outwardly, Sarah smiled as she led Katelynn back to the room where the ladies sat quilting, now discussing plans for another quilt project. As she set out a chair for Katelynn, she already knew of something she could do for Matthew, to help him, but a little.

Matthew set his mother's letter on the kitchen table. The page was filled, front and back, of Wolfesboro news, which, now that he had had some time in the much smaller town of Apple Creek, didn't seem all that interesting.

God help him, he still didn't know where he was supposed to be. The very act of living in Apple Creek wasn't as restrictive as Wolfesboro, but the atmosphere had not improved much, even after things seemed to have settled down with the farm stand incident, as some were calling it. He and Thad Graber continued to talk about the furniture store Thad hoped to open in Apple Creek, and Matthew had an inkling to be an investor, if not approach Thad outright about being a business partner. He had the funds, but was that what he really wanted to do?

Keith Donnelly had dropped the charge against Matthew. He'd been notified by way of a notice from the county court system. No explanation, other than that the hearing in December had been canceled and charges dropped. Of course, Matthew thanked God for that, but it didn't improve his situation in the community much. He didn't think they would care that an English judge had sent him a letter saying essentially that everything was now fine. The taint and distrust were still there. Maybe it always would be.

Midafternoon quiet had descended on the house. The Bylers were out visiting their daughter who had just given birth to a new baby. Mrs. Byler had put a chicken in the oven to roast, and Matthew had promised to keep an eye on it.

A soft knock on the front door sounded, so Matthew went to answer it. His heart leaped, and he felt a bit of a shock to see Sarah standing there. She held something covered with a cloth.

"Hello. I was hoping you would be here." Her brown eyes shone softly.

"Yes." He joined her on the porch. "The Bylers are not home."

"I'll stay right here then." She pulled the cloth off to reveal a still-warm pie. Apple, he judged by the luscious aroma that wafted in his direction. "This is to say thank you."

"Thank you?" He accepted the pie from her, their fingers brushing as he did so. He didn't regret the brief contact, which he realized he'd been longing for. If only things had been different. Were different. "Why are you thanking me?"

At the Bylers' encouraging, Matthew had attended Sunday services, despite any moments of discomfort he felt. It had become tolerable, but he was going to leave at Thanksgiving and stay with his parents in Wolfesboro after the holiday. Maybe for good.

Sarah cleared her throat. "I remembered what happened with Keith Donnelly that day. You helped me, and I'm very thankful you were there. So I wanted to say thank you."

"Would you like to have a piece of pie with me?" he heard himself asking.

"Right now?"

At that, Sarah smiled, glancing at the door as she did so. "Why, yes. Mother is seeing to supper, so I can stay. What about the Bylers?"

"We'll stay out here until they return. No one can say anything if we do not go inside alone, together. But I can get us plates and forks. And set coffee brewing, so we can enjoy it right here on the porch."

"All right. That sounds lovely."

Oh, how Matthew liked her smile. As he returned inside the house, part of him felt light as a cloud and the other part of him screeched a warning inside: *You're going to leave. Why spend time in this way, only to disappoint you both?*

He ignored the part of him screeching the inner warning and instead concentrated on lighting the stove's cooktop to get the coffee going. Then he fetched two plates, two forks, and a knife from the kitchen, and returned to the porch where Sarah sat on one of the two rocking chairs.

Matthew joined her and took the other empty rocking chair. Herbert had made both of them, he said, years ago when he was busy with a furniture-making endeavor.

"Here," Matthew said as he placed the plates on the short table between the chairs.

Sarah deftly sliced two pieces of pie and slipped one on each plate. "Enjoy."

The cinnamon, sweet-yet-tart filling made his taste buds dance. "This is delicious. One of the best I've ever had. Really."

"Danke. I couldn't think of another way to show my thanks." She paused, as if gathering her thoughts. "Matthew, I don't know if you've heard this or if it will help, but Keith has a lot of problems, from what his sister told me. He has not been taking his medication that controls his mental state and now he is in a lot of trouble himself."

Matthew nodded, slowly. "He dropped the charge against me, so the court says."

"Oh, that is very, very good to hear. I know that will help with the bishop and the elders in asking you to stay."

He set down his plate. "That's just it. I'm not sure I will stay. I am going to Wolfesboro for Thanksgiving, and I am not sure that I will be back."

"I see." Her face sank. "Well, I know it hasn't been easy for you with some of the talk. I wish people wouldn't."

Matthew shrugged. He'd resigned himself to the fact that people talk, and he couldn't control that. "Well, there was a woman I used to know who stopped by Abraham's farm a few weeks ago. She had some hard times when I knew her. Rebecca Mast. She is now doing very well."

Sarah nodded. "She's the young woman who brought her adopted son to visit you."

"Jah. We were close once. Just friends." He paused, clearing his throat. "But her son is not mine. That was, ah, a rumor."

"I did not think he was your son, but if he was, I know you would do the right thing by him. And now you've returned to us, to your plain people." She toyed with a bit of crust on her plate.

A buggy came barreling up the driveway and glided past Sarah's. The Bylers were back. While Herbert saw to the horse and buggy, Lavinia approached the porch. She carried a tote bag and wore a bemused expression.

If Lavinia wondered about Matthew sitting with an unmarried woman, alone on the front porch, she didn't say anything.

All she said was, "Oh, Sarah. So *gut* to see you. You'll stay for supper?" Her glance flicked to Matthew, and she smiled.

Sarah did indeed stay for supper, a hearty meal with roasted chicken, mashed potatoes with gravy, creamed corn, home-canned green beans, and biscuits straight from the oven. She liked the couple, who were about her parents' age but seemed younger, for some reason.

All the while, the conversation was light. They talked about her sister and Jacob's move to the new house, about preparations for winter and whether they would get much snow this year. No one talked about the farm stand incident, for which she was relieved. Now that she and Matthew had spoken about it, she wanted the matter to be behind them once and for all—despite the occasional bad dream she had about Keith chasing her through the garden, dreams she never told anyone about and didn't plan to. If she didn't give them voice, they would have no power over her.

"You are still planning to go to Wolfesboro then?" Herbert asked directly to Matthew. The atmosphere in the room deflated like a lump of bread dough sagging in the oven.

"Jah, I believe so." Matthew glanced to his right where Sarah sat. She held his gaze for a split-second.

"Nothing, then, to keep you here for the holidays?" Mrs. Byler asked gently.

"Well, I had hoped so. I had ideas, but evidently they weren't God's will for me." Matthew set down his fork.

"Maybe it just needs a little more time." Mrs. Byler rose from the table. "Dessert? I know you two have already had yours."

Sarah placed her napkin on the table. "Danke, jah, we have. I should leave before it's completely dark. It was a very, very good meal, and I enjoyed visiting you all."

"We will have to see you again sometime." Mrs. Byler took out some clean plates. "Thank you again for bringing the pie."

Sarah nodded, rising from her chair. She didn't think Mamm would worry if she was delayed, and would probably assume the Bylers had her stay to supper. Twilight had just begun to descend outside. She should be home in less than fifteen minutes.

Matthew stood as well. "I'll see you outside, Sarah."

She tried to ignore the feeling that prickled down her spine as he said her name. Once out the front door, she took a deep breath.

Matthew was right behind her. "Thank you again for stopping by."

Sarah turned to face him in the deepening twilight. "You are most welcome." She looked down to see her hand on his arm.

"Sarah—"

"Oh, Matthew . . . is there nothing that can convince you to stay? Nothing at all?" The thought of him leaving was breaking her heart.

"It's not as simple as me wanting to stay." He moved her hand from his arm and gripped it between his own. "I have never felt at home anywhere, for a long time. I was starting to think my place was in Apple Creek. But after losing a farm I never really had, and then everything else, I don't know. If the bishop and elders are leaning toward not accepting me, then I should go sooner than later."

"You are living under the roof of one of the elders right now. My Daed is not so angry as he once was," Sarah said. Her heart hammered in her chest as Matthew held her hand. "I believe he was simply afraid of anything happening to me, and when it did . . ."

Matthew looked into her eyes. "What about Jeremiah Hilty?"

"What of him?" Sarah heard her voice shaking. "I am not standing on his porch right now."

With that, she raised up on her tiptoes, planted a kiss on Matthew's cheek, then dashed to her buggy without a look back. What had she just done? As bold as it had been, she'd remember the feel of her lips on his cheek for the rest of her life.

17

Sarah was tired of rolling out dough. It was not one of her favorite baking tasks. At the moment, however, there were six crusts. Each pie would take about an hour to bake, so if she baked them three at a time they could have a dozen pies baked by lunchtime.

Tomorrow, she and Katelynn would prepare the fruit pies—apple, blueberry, and cherry—for the Thanksgiving farm stand sale.

Sarah had insisted that they do all the baking in her family's own kitchen, to which Mamm agreed, since all she would have to cook were vegetables and dressing on Thanksgiving morning, before the afternoon meal. The Stoltzfuses would all be gathering on Thanksgiving Day at Jacob and Emma's home, the former Miller farm.

She glanced at the clock on the kitchen wall. Almost seven o'clock, and the oven would soon be hot enough to put the first pies in the oven. Katelynn was due any moment and would be bringing the filling, insisting on making the process go faster with an electric mixer, for which Sarah was secretly grateful.

Mamm was over at Emma's home, getting the house set up, now that the sale had been completed.

Footsteps and a loud bumping noise came from the porch, then a soft knock. Sarah hurried to the door and opened it. Katelynn stood there clutching the handle of a cooler with wheels.

"Good morning, come in. I've almost got the first few crusts prepared." Sarah motioned in the direction of the kitchen. "All you'll have to do is pour, then we can get the pies baking."

Katelynn rolled the cooler through the front room, then glanced around. "Every time I come here I can't help but think how cute your house is. So simply decorated and so uncluttered and clean. Except for last time. I was so upset about Keith, I didn't pay much attention."

Her friend seemed in better spirits than the last time she'd seen her, even at the mention of her brother. Well, keeping busy was good medicine, and Katelynn certainly had plenty to do.

"I've got the pie filling ready to go," Katelynn continued. "It's in containers, on ice, because I didn't know how long it would sit."

"Good idea. I did not think of that." Sarah helped Katelynn remove the first plastic container of pumpkin pie mixture from the cooler. After the pies were completed and cooled, Katelynn would take them home to the refrigerator in her mother's garage. They would keep well until Wednesday, when the customers—the last ones they would ever have—had been told to come by the stand to pick up their pie orders.

Within a few minutes, the first of the pumpkin pies were filled and baking. Katelynn took a seat on one of the chairs.

Katelynn's bright mood dissipated now that the flurry of activity was over for now. "About my brother . . ." Katelynn's eyes filled with tears. "I am so, so sorry for everything he did. How he hurt you, and what he did to Matthew . . ." She shook her head, and the tears spilled down her cheeks.

"Oh, Katelynn." Sarah took the seat opposite her friend. "I forgive him. I must. There is no other way for me. If I were to harbor anger at him, or at you, it would be wrong. God has forgiven me, so I must forgive others."

"I know that's what you believe. It's just hard to understand sometimes. It's going to be a long, long time before I trust him ever again."

Sarah did understand that. "There is a time to be wise as a serpent and harmless like a dove. I believe that is true in this case. He will always be your brother."

"Well, I want you to know he's come home again. And he's now getting help. He's going away for a while again, after this weekend. There's a program the court referred him to. It'll be quite a long time, but I'm hoping he'll be on his way to having a good life again."

"That is my prayer for him, as well." Sarah stood. "Would you like some coffee?"

"I would love some, with cream and sugar if you have it."

"We have both." Sarah went to the stove where the coffee sat, still warm from the heat of the oven beneath. She poured them both a cup, then picked up the cream and sugar containers.

"Thank you." Katelynn stirred her coffee, casting a glance at Sarah as she did so. "Have you heard anything more from Matthew—anything at all?"

A week had passed since the evening on the porch and her very-forward, impulsive kiss.

"He is staying with Herbert Byler and his wife, now that Jacob and Emma have moved. I saw him the other evening, at the Bylers' home, in fact." Sarah added some cream to her coffee and stirred.

"Is there any hope for him to stay in your community?"

Her throat grew thick with emotion. "I really don't know. No one has asked him to leave. But he might leave anyway. Abraham has gone to Florida, and Matthew knows he can find work there."

Sarah did not tell Katelynn about the pie she made him, to thank him, nor the kiss she gave him after hearing he might leave Apple Creek. That was a memory she wanted to keep all to herself.

The aroma of baking pumpkin and savory crust filled the kitchen, which was silent except for the ticking of the wall clock.

"I wish people would give him a chance," Katelynn said.

"I do too. But if he's not happy here he must go. It has been hard for him with all the speculation and rumors flying about unfairly. We talk about forgiveness and grace, but we don't always practice it."

"But if Keith deserves grace, then so does Matthew."

"Oh, I know he does, and I believe it. It's wrong what rumors can do to people, harming relationships and more. I don't know what would have happened if he hadn't tried to defend me." At her friend's stricken look, she added, "I'm sorry, Katelynn. I shouldn't have said that. But I'm okay, and Keith's getting help. I'm grateful for both those things."

"Me too," Katelynn's eyes had misted over again. "I'm just glad we're still friends."

"Of course we are. Now let's talk about something else." Conversation then turned to baking, Thanksgiving, Christmas, and Katelynn's wedding, which Sarah had been meaning to bring up.

"Katelynn, about my being a bridesmaid in your wedding. I never did talk to the bishop about it, but I don't need to. As much as I would love to support you, I would feel uncomfortable in such a role, although I would like to attend the ceremony as a guest. I am so very sorry if I am disappointing you."

Katelynn didn't seem surprised, and smiled. "Don't worry about that at all. I should have thought about your feelings before I asked, but I was so excited about the wedding and all. Since then I've realized you might not want to or be able to be one of my attendants. So I have another request."

Sarah blew out a soft breath of relief. She hadn't realized quite how heavily that decision had been weighing on her heart, even though she knew it was the right one. "Please ask. If it's in my power, you know I will help you."

"I can't believe I didn't think of this before anyway. Would you read a scripture passage during the ceremony? Would that be okay?" Katelynn's face was hopeful.

Read in front of an English church full of people? She consulted her heart. It took only a moment to know that Gött would want her to give this couple the benefit of His words, and He had put the idea into Katelynn's head. Who was she to argue? Gött would give her courage when the time came.

"I would be honored and thankful that I can serve Him in that way," she said.

Katelynn let out a squeal of delight.

In spite of the events this fall, Sarah realized she did have a lot to be thankful for, including the all-too-brief time she'd had with Matthew. Whether he stayed or left, the matter was now in Gött's hands.

Sunday morning came, and with it, another service, this one at Emma and Jacob's farm, the first for the young couple.

Matthew almost didn't want to go, but Herbert urged him to attend the service with his head held high, like he had for the past several meetings.

Herbert also made an announcement after bringing the buggy around to the front of the house.

"I'm tired of all the talebearing," Herbert said as Matthew donned his hat. "It does not honor our Gött, and it causes divisions among us. You, Matthew, have been divided from us by talebearing, not by your own actions."

"Thank you, Herbert." Matthew slipped his arms into his warm coat and fastened its belt. It was a hand-me-down from Abraham, who said he wouldn't need it in Florida.

"I quite agree, Herbert." Lavinia put on her own winter coat. "I believe idleness is a talebearer's worst weakness. If they were not idle and were minding their own business, they would not have time to gossip."

The older couple's support buoyed his spirits as they traveled the two miles to the new Stoltzfus farm. Which could have been his farm.

Yet, the more he thought about it and recalled his conversation with Sarah last week, it seemed his time here in Apple Creek was at an end. There would be no construction jobs nearby this winter. He wanted to earn his keep and not be a burden to anyone.

The community gathered in the barn today, with its snug, repaired roof and relative warmth. Matthew received a few greetings, which was encouraging, especially after Herbert's words of support on the ride here. But nothing was changed, not really. Jacob passed him by without a word, but Matthew paid it no mind as the men and women divided up into their respective sides of the barn.

Halfway through the first hymn, an English man walked into the barn. Curious looks replaced expressions of worship as the singers fell silent.

A knot formed in Matthew's chest. What was Keith Donnelly doing here?

Keith looked far different than the last time Matthew had encountered the man, that horrible day at the farm stand. He wore a clean jacket, dark pants, and a vivid red shirt with buttons and a collar. His hair and facial hair were neatly trimmed.

He looked almost like a cardinal among crows, standing against the black and white of the Amish. He also looked uncomfortable, as if he were ready to run.

Keith squared his shoulders and headed straight for the bishop, stopping in front of the man.

Bishop wasn't happy, but said, "Good morning. Why have you interrupted our service?"

"Good morning, ah, Reverend." Keith's head bobbed. "I gather you're the main preacher here today?"

"I am the bishop."

Keith glanced around at the plain people watching him. He looked directly at Matthew, who stared unflinchingly back at him. The man had some nerve, barging in like that.

"Ah, I wanted to say something, in front of everyone, if that is all right. I, ah, won't take long. I promise." He wrung his hands. "It's, ah, a confession, I want to tell everyone."

"You may speak," said the bishop.

Matthew still didn't know what the man was up to. Keith Donnelly had a world of problems, and they had caught up with him, that was for certain.

"All right." Keith turned to face the group. "My name is Keith Donnelly, and I have a problem. It's a mental disorder, and I need help dealing with it. When I see a doctor and take my medicine, I do okay. That might not mean much to some of you, but I know that the things I've done when I wasn't getting help have hurt some people in this room. For that, I ask forgiveness. I tried to steal from Miss Sarah's cashbox. Well, it was my sister's too.

"I also hurt Miss Sarah. It was an accident. But I didn't know what I was doing. All I knew was I needed money. Or thought I did. I knew Miss Sarah had plenty of cash at the stand. But she wouldn't give me any. I got angry and scared her. It was a mistake. It was wrong. I pushed her, then she fell and got hurt.

"Then when Matthew stuck up for her, I tried to make him fight me. I was the one trying to hit him. My sister tells me y'all don't fight, and you think it's wrong. Well, I was wrong to lie to the deputy when I told them Matthew was the one who attacked me. I'd probably want to punch someone who threatened my girl, so I don't blame him for wanting to. Not a bit. But he didn't do anything except try to get out of my way."

Murmurs rose up from the group, followed by whispers. Bishop Hilty raised his hand for silence. Matthew was stunned. Sarah wasn't "his girl," but the confession alone had him unable to make a sound.

Keith continued.

"I'm almost done. After that, I was arrested for trying to rob a store. I got caught. The courts are sending me away, to get help with my problem. I don't know if y'all knew about that part. But I wanted y'all to hear it from me. It's the truth. I'm really sorry."

With that, Keith turned to leave the barn.

Sarah stood. "Wait. Keith Donnelly, I forgive you."

Matthew found himself following suit. "As do I."

Keith ran from the barn, and the sound of a car engine leaving soon followed.

The bishop cleared his throat as both Sarah and Matthew took their seats.

"I believe that now is as good a time as any to give today's message on reconciliation."

After the service, a few approached Matthew, offering their apologies and firm handshakes. Herbert patted him on the shoulder, a twinkle in his eye.

Matthew caught sight of the bishop motioning him to join him near the barn door, after most of those in attendance had filed out. Standing nearby was Sarah, along with her parents.

"I've made a decision that I know Herbert will agree with, but I wanted Levi to hear, and you, too, Matthew. I'm going to recommend that you be given full membership in our district, at the start of the new year."

Matthew felt a bit numb. After all that had happened, acceptance? Just like that? Sarah looked at him with shining eyes.

He should not question the gift. "Danke, Bishop."

Levi also gave his own nod. "I agree as well. I'm afraid I was harsh with you, Matthew. It wasn't fair. You were a good neighbor and a good caregiver for Abraham. Better than I was, and I lived beside him for years. Please forgive me."

"Of course I forgive you." Matthew knew the man's anger had come from being protective of Sarah, his daughter.

"Do you think you'll stay, after all?" Sarah asked. "Please stay, Matthew."

Emboldened, he took her hands in his, heedless of the people standing around. "I'll stay if you'll let me court you. I have plans to work, and work hard, here in Apple Creek. Or I could also get work in Florida, if it comes to that."

"One thing at a time, Matthew," Levi said. But despite his serious tone, the man had warmth in his eyes. "And you may court my daughter, not that you asked. Sarah, what do you say?"

Sarah's smile widened. "I say yes."

Sarah's mother fanned herself. "Oh, another one leaving Apple Creek." "Oh, Mamm," Sarah said. "Not necessarily. But wherever I go, this place will always be my home."

Epilogue

The air was almost balmy for January in Tennessee, just warm enough for the double wedding of Thad and Lydia Graber, and Matthew and Sarah Miller.

Not every friend would be so gracious to share her day with another woman, but that's what Lydia did, and Sarah was thankful for it.

What a wondrous day it had been yesterday, marrying Matthew with their friends and family around them all. Sarah would remember it as long as she lived. He had been baptized, not two weeks before.

After both couples returned from their wedding trips, the new owners of Graber & Miller Amish Furniture would continue to work toward a grand opening.

Sarah and Matthew would stay here with Mamm and Daed until their new home was completed in the spring. Her Daed had been very generous, giving them a few acres of land from the old Miller property, so a piece of it at least was staying in the Miller family. Matthew had been touched when Daed told them, and still seemed to be in a state of wonderment over all the changes that happened in just a few short months.

Well, it *was* pretty wonderful, wasn't it?

Sarah glanced at the large suitcase by the front door. Their driver would be here soon, paid for with some of Sarah's savings. She had insisted to Matthew that she wanted to pay for part of the trip to Florida.

"Are you ready?" Matthew enveloped her in an embrace. Oh, it felt so good to hold him and to be held.

"I am ready and have been ever since you told me about Pinecraft."

At that, he smiled. "Abraham is looking forward to seeing us. I called him from the general store. He is very good at using a phone now."

"Imagine that." Sarah was too excited to think of phones at the moment.

A honk sounded outside. The driver!

Sarah had already bid her Daed farewell at breakfast, but knew she needed to say another goodbye to her Mamm and to Emma, and to give her new nephew one more cuddle. Two weeks was a long time to be gone from the only home, the only place she'd ever known.

As if sensing her thoughts, Matthew said, "We can stop by your sister's house to say goodbye."

"How long is the car ride going to be?"

"Hours and hours. But they'll go by quickly, I promise." Matthew caressed her face.

"Yes, they will. Especially if you sing to me. The driver won't mind."

He hugged her tighter. "From now on, every song I sing will be for you."

Up to this point, we've been doing all the writing. Now it's *your* turn!

Tell us what you think about this book, the characters, the plot, or anything else you'd like to share with us about this series. We can't wait to hear from *you*!

Log on to give us your feedback at:
https://www.surveymonkey.com/r/HeartsOfAmish

Annie's® FICTION